Margaret Cho: Comedian, Actress, and Activist

✴ Influential Asians ✴

MARGARET CHO

Comedian, Actress, and Activist

Michael A. Schuman

Enslow Publishing
101 W. 23rd Street
Suite 240
New York, NY 10011
USA

enslow.com

Published in 2017 by Enslow Publishing, LLC.
101 W. 23rd Street, Suite 240, New York, NY 10011

Copyright © 2017 by Enslow Publishing, LLC.

All rights reserved.

No part of this book may be reproduced by any means without the written permission of the publisher.

Library of Congress Cataloging-in-Publication Data

Names: Schuman, Michael, author.
Title: Margaret Cho : comedian, actress, and activist / Michael A. Schuman.
Description: New York, NY : Enslow Publishing, 2017. | Series: Influential Asians | Includes bibliographical references and index.
Identifiers: LCCN 2015050613 | ISBN 9780766079045 (library bound)
Subjects: LCSH: Cho, Margaret—Juvenile literature. | Comedians—United States—Biography—Juvenile literature. | Asian American comedians—Biography—Juvenile literature.
Classification: LCC PN2287.C537 S37 2016 | DDC 792.702/8092—dc23
LC record available at http://lccn.loc.gov/2015050613

Printed in the United States of America

To Our Readers: We have done our best to make sure all websites in this book were active and appropriate when we went to press. However, the author and the publisher have no control over and assume no liability for the material available on those websites or on any websites they may link to. Any comments or suggestions can be sent by e-mail to customerservice@enslow.com.

Photo Credits: Cover, p. 3 Andrew Toth/Getty Images Entertainment/Getty Images; p. 6 Angela Weiss/Getty Images Entertainment/Getty Images; p. 12 Robyn Beck/AFP/Getty Images; p. 14 Jeff Kravitz/FilmMagic, Inc/Getty Images; p. 21 Seth Poppel Yearbook Library; p. 24 Webbi1987/Wikimedia Commons/SFSU Campus JPL Library Nov2012.JPG/CC-BY-SA-3.0; p. 29 Ron Galella, Ltd./Getty Images; p. 31 Time & Life Pictures/The LIFE Picture Collection/Getty Images; p. 35 David Buchan/Getty Images Entertainment/Getty Images; p. 37 Everett Collection; p. 41 Christopher Polk/Getty Images Entertainment/Getty Images; p. 44 Hulton Archive/Getty Images; p. 46 © AF archive/Alamy; p. 51 Katy Winn/Getty Images Entertainment/Getty Images; pp. 57, 71, 110 Kevin Winter/Getty Images Entertainment/Getty Images; p. 67 Rick Kern/WireImage/Getty Images; p. 69 David Paul Morris/Getty Images News/Getty Images; p. 76 Chris Weeks/Hulton Archive/Getty Images; p. 81 Michael Schwartz/WireImage/Getty Images; p. 82 Gary Friedman/Los Angeles Times/Getty Images; p. 84 Richard Hartog/Los Angeles Times/Getty Images; p. 87 © Cho Taussig/courtesy Everett Collection; p. 89 Frazer Harrison/Getty Images Entertainment/Getty Images; p. 93 Justin Sullivan/Getty Images News/Getty Images; p. 96 Tim Mosenfelder/Getty Images Entertainment/Getty Images; p. 99 David McNew/Getty Images News/Getty Images; p. 100 Alberto E. Rodriguez/Getty Images Entertainment/Getty Images; p. 104 Frederick M. Brown/Getty Images Entertainment/Getty Images; p. 107 Handout/Getty Images Entertainment/Getty Images.

Contents

1. A Wonderful Mother's Day Present 7
2. "They Hated Me" 11
3. Joking Around with Batwing Lubricant 26
4. All-American Girl 38
5. Too Asian or Not Asian Enough 49
6. "This Isn't Me. This Is Stupid." 61
7. Lining Up Around the Block 73
8. "I Got Squid and Peanuts" 83
9. The Activist 91
10. Pride 102

Chronology 112
Chapter Notes 114
Glossary 122
Further Reading 124
Index 126

Margaret Cho turned the pain she felt from being marginalized into comedy.

Chapter 1

A Wonderful Mother's Day Present

In 1994, Margaret Cho was a successful stand-up comedian. She headlined comedy shows in nightclubs and on college campuses. She also appeared in minor roles on television shows and movies. But like many comedians, Cho's big dream was to star in her own situation comedy. A situation comedy is a television show that runs regularly, usually once a week. It involves the same characters every week in different stories. *The Big Bang Theory* and *Modern Family* are situation comedies. Sometimes people call them sitcoms for short.

Cho's agent and manager both decided the time had come for Cho to star in a sitcom of her own. At first she had no idea what the show should be about other than it would feature an Asian-American family living in the United States. Many of Margaret's favorite television shows when she was growing up were broadcast on the ABC television network. These included classic family fare such as *Fantasy Island*, *The Love Boat*, and *Charlie's Angels*.

While Margaret liked those shows, they all had one thing in common. There were few if any Asians on them. The few Asian characters that were on television shows were mostly stereotypes, such as a loyal servant or a Chinese restaurant owner. It made her feel left out, as if something was wrong with people like her. She hoped her show would correct those past wrongs. It would be the first one on a major television network that had an Asian-American family as its main characters.

The executives at ABC came up with an idea for the theme of her new show. Margaret would play a twenty-one-year-old rebellious girl growing up with conservative Korean parents. It wasn't that much different from her real life. It would be called *All-American Girl*.

The Pilot

The first step was to make a test episode, known in television business as a pilot. Just because a pilot had been made, that didn't mean *All-American Girl* would be chosen to be televised. Television networks make more pilots than they will have room for on their schedule.

A Wonderful Mother's Day Present

Some pilots just don't work. They might include comedies that people don't find funny. Some might be dramas that people don't find engaging.

In order to test the show, the producers played the pilot for an audience of ABC executives. They wanted the executives' opinions on the show. Then they played it for focus groups.

Focus Groups

There are different kinds of focus groups. In the television business, a focus group is a selection of average citizens hired to watch television pilots before anyone else. They offer their opinions of the pilot to network executives. If enough people in the focus group like it, chances are it will be televised on the network in the future. The creator of the idea of a focus group was Robert K. Merton. He was a professor and sociologist, or a person who studies the way people interact with one another. Most focus groups include eight to ten people.

The announcements regarding which pilots would be made into television series were to be made public at a big ceremony in New York City on a Sunday in May 1994. Margaret flew to New York to attend the event.

After an afternoon of shopping, she had just returned to her hotel room when the telephone rang. It was a call from one of the ABC staff members. The network said yes—it decided to put *All-American Girl* on their fall schedule. The producers were given the go-ahead to make thirteen episodes.

This was the first step toward making Margaret's personal dream come true. It happened to be Mother's Day, so the first thing Margaret did was call her mother in San Francisco. She was thrilled to hear Margaret's exciting news. It was a wonderful Mother's Day present. "It was the miracle I had been waiting all my life for," Margaret said.[1]

Chapter 2

"THEY HATED ME"

Margaret Moran Cho was born on December 5, 1968, in San Francisco, California. Her middle name, Moran, is Korean and translates to "peony flower." The peony is a plant known for its hardiness. It can be red, pink, or white and looks similar to a carnation.

Margaret was raised in an unusual but busy urban neighborhood called Haight-Ashbury (pronounced like "hate"). It is named that because the corner of Haight and Ashbury streets is one of the neighborhood's main intersections.

Margaret's parents were immigrants from Seoul, the capital of South Korea. Humor ran in the Cho family.

Cho grew up in San Francisco's famed Haight-Ashbury neighborhood. Haight-Ashbury was the center of hippie activity in the 1960s and continues to be associated with the counterculture.

Margaret's father was a successful writer of joke books in Korean. Margaret later said, "I guess we're in the same line of work."[1] However, she always thought her father's jokes were corny even though other people laughed heartily at them.

When Margaret was born, Haight-Ashbury was in a neighborhood known all across the country. Rebellious people in their late teens and early twenties were moving from all parts of the United States to her neighborhood. They were part of a movement called the hippies.

"They Hated Me"

When Margaret was just three days old, her father was deported, or sent back, to Korea. Margaret never understood exactly why. It most likely had to do with the country's laws about the settlement of immigrants. Whatever the reason, Margaret's father was scared to tell her mother that he was being deported. He waited until the day he was actually being deported to let her know. He would come back, but for now, his future was uncertain.

Margaret's mother did not want to raise her baby daughter in a one-parent home. Soon afterwards, she moved with Margaret into an apartment where Margaret's

The Hippie Movement

In the 1940s and 1950s a person aware of the latest nontraditional trends was called "hep." By the mid-1960s the word "hep" had morphed into "hip." People who were hip became known as hippies. There were hippies in all parts of the country, but San Francisco's Haight-Ashbury neighborhood was their unofficial capital.

Hippies rejected many of their parents' values. To them, it was their parents' rigid ideas that led to American involvement in the unpopular Vietnam War. Hippies wanted to look and act as differently as possible from their parents' generation. They grew their hair long. They experimented with illegal drugs and embraced rock music. Rock was still fairly young and one thing that made it popular among hippies is that many of their parents hated it.

aunt and uncle lived. They owned a convenience store in the Nob Hill section of San Francisco.

Despite the unusual living situation, Margaret's mother tried to raise her as normally as possible. She sent Margaret to the nearby Notre Dame Nursery School, which was run by the Catholic Church. Margaret's mother often dropped her off at her aunt and uncle's store after nursery school so she could run errands.

Margaret's parents had emigrated to the United States from Korea. When her husband was temporarily deported, Margaret's mother moved them into an apartment with other family.

Always in Trouble

Margaret seemed to have trouble staying on good behavior. She got in trouble for doing things like dabbing finger paint on one of her classmates and crawling around on the floor when she was supposed to be napping. She was often sent to the office of Mother Superior (the head of the school) as punishment. But Mother Superior wasn't that tough. She would usually look at Margaret and smile before sending her on her way.

One December the school was planning a Christmas pageant. All the kids' parents were invited. The children were scheduled to sing a Christmas song as a group. The teachers were concerned that the children might wave to their parents if they saw their parents waving from the audience. Their concern was that if one child started waving, the others might do so, too. That could ruin the pageant.

As soon as Margaret went on stage with her classmates, she looked into the audience. Sure enough, her mother and aunt were waving to her. Margaret was torn. On the one hand, she didn't want to disobey her teachers. On the other hand, she didn't want to disappoint her mother and aunt.

Before she knew it, Margaret was raising her hand and waving to her family. An older boy noticed Margaret waving and he figured it would be nice to wave to his family, too. Almost right away, a third child waved. Before long, the entire class onstage were waving to their friends and family. Being so young, the children lost their concentration. They weren't sure what song to sing. In desperation, the teachers led them off the stage.

Surprisingly, Margaret wasn't punished. In the confusion, the children simply left the school building with their families to go home for winter break. When everyone returned to school in January, it was as if the pageant disaster never happened. Nobody said anything about it. The teacher went back to teaching class.

Because of the botched pageant, Margaret learned something that would help her later on in life. When someone onstage waves to the audience, people in the audience will wave back.

When Margaret was five, her brother was born. The apartment the Chos were living in became awfully crowded. So they moved to their own house. To help Margaret's mother raise two small children, Margaret's grandparents moved from Korea to the Cho family's house. Her father returned from South Korea and her parents took a new job running a snack bar in a bowling alley. Margaret enjoyed eating the hamburgers her parents cooked. She enjoyed so many of them that she became a large child.

Trying to Fit In

Although she attended a religious nursery school, Margaret was enrolled in a public elementary school, the Dudley Stone School, for kindergarten. Like her home, it was located in Haight-Ashbury. By this time, the neighborhood had changed somewhat. The hippie movement was dying out.

"They Hated Me"

However, there were some hippies who never left. Many had drug addictions and no jobs. The Haight had gone from a center of love and peace to a run-down neighborhood. Others living in the Haight were immigrants from China, Japan, and other Asian countries. There was also a sizable gay and lesbian community.

Among this human mosaic was small Margaret Moran Cho, trying to find a place to fit in. She was unpopular with the children her age. The kids picked on her for any mistake they saw her make.

When she was eight, Margaret was practicing for another Christmas program when she awkwardly dropped a rare and expensive brass bell. It fell to the floor and shattered into pieces. During another Christmas pageant rehearsal, she accidentally urinated on the floor after a teacher wouldn't allow her to leave the room. During recess most of the other children avoided her. Those who didn't ignore her insulted her. They constantly reminded her of the two embarrassing incidents that happened when she was eight.

Things were no better at church. Every Sunday her parents took her to services at the Korean Methodist Church. Again, Margaret had trouble fitting in. Cho said about the church, "They *hated* me there. Everyone. From the babies all the way to the teenagers. Maybe the teachers and the young pastor didn't, because they'd spend time trying to protect me and involve me in some activities, the same ones the other kids would try to

Margaret Cho: Comedian, Actress, and Activist

exclude me from. I don't think anyone could have been more hated. School was bad enough, but now it seemed like the whole world was a hostile place."[2]

As she grew into her preteen years, Margaret often dreamed about being someone else. She thought she would be happier if she were white. She fantasized that she was blonde and pretty like Lori Loughlin or Charlene Tilton. Loughlin and Tilton were actresses on popular television shows at that time.

Taunting at Church

Yet the kids who were meanest to her were not white but Korean like her. The most painful experiences happened at church. Much of the taunting stemmed from her Korean middle name, Moran. Her parents gave it to her because it represented strength and beauty. Yet the kids at the church turned Moran into "moron." Sometimes they said they couldn't see because Moron's fat head was in the way. Kids sitting near her would try to get away from her.

Despite the fact that she wasn't well liked at school or church, she did have two good friends she knew through her parents. Her parents were best friends with another Korean family, the Parks. The Parks had two daughters, Lotte and Connie. Margaret spent many days at the Park family home. Margaret, Lotte, and Connie spent time together shopping, listening to music, and watching television. Sometimes, Connie's shy female cousin, Ronny, would join them.

"They Hated Me"

During the summer when Margaret was twelve, she went away for three days on a church retreat. It was supposed to be a break from the noise and concrete sidewalks of the city. She was hoping to spend time with Lotte, Connie, and Ronny. Shortly after she arrived at camp, she walked by herself to the lake. Waiting there were two boys she knew from church. They immediately began picking on her, calling her moron just like they had done at home. She knew they didn't like her so their comments came as no surprise.

What was surprising was that Lotte, Connie, and Ronny joined the boys and repeatedly insulted Margaret. Just a few weeks earlier, the three girls and Margaret were the best of friends. She couldn't believe they turned on her and joined ranks with her enemies. She walked by herself back to her cabin. As Margaret sat down by herself on her sleeping bag, she heard a loud, crunching sound. Then she heard some girls laughing outside her cabin. Right away she recognized the voices of Lotte and Connie. Her former friends had filled Margaret's sleeping bag with dirt, leaves, garbage, and manure.

Margaret assumed that one of the church leaders must have talked to the other campers because nobody bothered her for the rest of the weekend. On the other hand, nobody wanted to be with her. No one would sit with her at mealtimes, nor would they sit near her by campfires. The girls who were supposed to share her bunk decided they would rather sleep on floor mats.

Margaret Cho: Comedian, Actress, and Activist

When she arrived home after the retreat ended, Margaret discovered that her father was not there. Her mother never explained where he was. Margaret told her mother she refused to go to that church again. Although her mother pleaded with her every Sunday morning to give the church one more try, Margaret refused. She couldn't stand the idea of spending one more minute around kids that were so vicious.

A Colorful Community

Her father returned home without any explanation of where he had been. He and Margaret's mother sold the snack bar to a relative. They decided to try a new business and opened a bookstore called Paperback Traffic. It was located on Polk Street in a neighborhood that had a large population of gay men.

The idea of homosexuality was foreign to Margaret. When she saw two men walking together she assumed they were good friends. When she saw them buying makeup, she figured it was for their girlfriends.

Some of the men who worked in Margaret's parents' bookstore were gay. By hanging around the bookstore during her leisure time, she got to know them very well. Even though they were older than her, they became her close friends. Perhaps because they were used to being outsiders, they didn't judge Margaret or make fun of her the way others did. Whenever she had questions about what it was like to be gay, they patiently answered them.

When she was fifteen, Margaret started attending Lowell High School. Lowell was a special high school

"They Hated Me"

for teens that had proven above average intelligence. But Margaret did not relate to the other kids. She thought the girls were mean and catty and the boys acted like she didn't exist. Cutting classes became routine for her. She spent most of her time hanging around with other class cutters, who spent most days drinking alcohol and smoking pot. Margaret rode the school bus every

As a teenager, Margaret had trouble fitting in at school and church. She began cutting classes and experimenting with drugs at an early age.

morning so her parents had no reason to believe that she wasn't attending school.

Some of the kids she hung around with actually did make efforts to catch up on homework assignments and show up for tests. But not Margaret. Of course, she couldn't get away with that forever. Her report card showed Fs in every subject except for one—and in that one she got a grade of incomplete. Her grade point average was 0.6 out of a possible 4.0. The school administration had no choice but to punish her. She wasn't merely suspended, however, she was expelled. She said, "My parents were so ashamed that they practically disowned me."[3] They had always emphasized the importance of education. They told her they sacrificed to make sure she got into good schools.

Finding the Theater

As embarrassing as it was to Margaret and her family, getting expelled was a wake-up call. She was getting tired of loafing and smoking pot all day. She learned that San Francisco State College was offering a summer stock theater program for high school students.

Margaret was smart enough to realize she would never get into college with her pathetic school record. However, this theater program was an exception. They did not care about her grades. They only cared whether she had talent. Unlike the classes at Lowell, theater classes intrigued her. And deep down, Margaret thought she could be a good performer.

"They Hated Me"

Summer Stock Theater

Summer stock theater refers to theater companies that present plays mainly between early or mid-June into September. Many are located in beach or mountain resorts. Several present their plays outdoors in order to take advantage of the warm weather. Three of the best known are Ogunquit Playhouse in Ogunquit, Maine; The Barnstormers in Tamworth, New Hampshire; and the Rocky Mountain Repertory Theater in Grand Lake, Colorado. The name combines the season with the tradition of these theaters' frequent uses of stock scenery. Stock scenery is scene-making material that can be used for different plays. Many of the actors in summer stock are beginners getting experience. However, quite a few are actors who have been in the business for years.

As before, Margaret didn't fit in right away with the other students in the theater program. She found many of the other students spoiled and immature. But then she met a fellow student named Claudia. Like Margaret, Claudia was an outcast. Claudia was into punk rock and had a shaved head. Margaret discovered she and Claudia liked the same music.

Through Claudia, she met another student named Lauren. They got along very well and hung around together even after summer was over. Margaret felt she finally had some true friends. She confessed, "I'd never felt closer to anyone. I felt loved and accepted,

Margaret Cho: Comedian, Actress, and Activist

just as myself. We laughed a lot. We didn't even need drugs then."[4]

Margaret had planned to attend a public high school in the fall. But another friend from the theater group named Alexi told Margaret she would be attending the School of the Arts (SOTA). Alexi suggested that Margaret audition for a spot at SOTA.

Cho decided to try a summer theater program sponsored by San Francisco State. Aside from igniting her passion for performing, the program introduced her to her first true friends.

Margaret did and was accepted. At SOTA, she still had to take classes in standard school subjects such as English and math. But much of her time was spent in acting workshops. She had a lot in common with the kids known as the arts freaks. She joined a student comedy group that acted in sketches for the students and teachers. Margaret admitted that performing onstage felt like the most natural thing in the world. She said, "I don't know what I would have done if I hadn't gone there. I was pretty desperate, seeing as I was kicked out of school, and it was a great way to learn about what eventually became my profession."[5]

Chapter 3

JOKING AROUND WITH BATWING LUBRICANT

For the first time as a teenager, Margaret took school seriously. She enjoyed the classes and students at SOTA. Bad report cards were a thing of the past. She knew she had to have good grades in order to stay eligible for the theater program.

Although Margaret had had little success in school, she was very intelligent. But she was also street smart. Much of that had to do with growing up in a big, diverse city.

Big-city living is generally tougher and more complicated than suburban or small-town living. "Street smart" means being able to get by in tough situations. Cities are home to both very rich people and very poor ones. There are homeless people living on the streets. Generous people often give money to the homeless to help them. But some people begging for money are not homeless—or poor. They simply find it easier to depend on the kindness of strangers rather than work. And while many of the poor use that money to buy food or clothing, others are addicts who spend it on alcohol and illegal drugs. Drug dealing is commonplace in some city neighborhoods.

The Dark Side

Margaret started hanging around with a group of people older than her. One of her best friends was named Duncan. Duncan didn't have a regular job. He also didn't have a permanent home. He drifted from job to job and apartment to apartment. But he was good to Margaret. They never dated, but they had fun times together.

Although Margaret had quit smoking pot, before long she was using heavier drugs. She confessed, "I called up Duncan in Berkeley one night and begged him to come into San Francisco and score some speed. He heard an urgency in my voice that frightened him. He wouldn't do it. Because he didn't, I realize now that he probably saved my life. He made me see that my hobby was turning into a full-fledged jones."[1] ["Jones" is a slang term for an addiction.]

It was through Duncan that Margaret met a man named Bob. He was twenty-six years old. Even though Margaret was just sixteen, she and Bob started dating. Despite their age difference, Margaret often seemed the more mature person in the couple. After a while she started to lose interest in Bob. It became hard for her to deal with his lack of maturity.

Margaret kept seeing Bob for some time because she didn't have the heart to break up with him. But she knew they weren't right for each other. She met him in a coffee house on Haight Street and tried to gently break up. But Bob's reaction was to yell at her. He insulted her and all Koreans. Despite Bob's mean words, Margaret felt a sense of pride. She said it was the first time in her life she had stood up for herself.[2]

But it wasn't long before Margaret was back into her bad drug habits. She began smoking marijuana again. One side effect of marijuana is food cravings. The more she smoked pot the more she ate. And the more she ate the more weight she gained.

She was also using heavier drugs. She knew her drug habit was putting her on a destructive path.[3] Then she found that doing comedy onstage was a temporary way to control her drug use. She knew she couldn't be under the influence of drugs and perform well at the same time.

Finding a Home in Comedy Clubs

Margaret and some friends from her high school comedy troupe, Batwing Lubricant, started skipping classes again. But instead of bumming around, they spent time

Joking Around with Batwing Lubricant

Plagued by bad relationships and a drug habit, Cho finally found a place where she belonged: the comedy clubs.

in comedy clubs to watch professional comedians do their acts. One of Margaret's favorites was The Punchline. She liked to sit in the audience and observe the people onstage.

Being a professional comedian involves much more than telling funny jokes. One needs a good delivery, or manner of talking to the audience, so the jokes don't fall flat. It is also important to have a sharp sense of timing, so the audience can appreciate one joke before the comedian goes on to his or her next one. That takes practice. Try telling a story to your friends and family without interrupting yourself by saying things like, "um," "ah," and "you know." It's difficult. An audience will lose its attention if a comedian does that.

So she could spend as much time as possible in the comedy clubs, Margaret dropped out of SOTA in her senior year. In a way, the clubs became her new classrooms.

Club owners saw her and her friends there so often that one finally allowed Batwing Lubricant to do a show. They took the stage at a famous club called The Other Café. The Other Café is known as the place where the legendary comedian Robin Williams often performed. Although Batwing Lubricant consisted of teenagers, they were a huge hit. The club owner invited them to return to do another show.

But Margaret was restless. Even though she was getting good exposure in San Francisco, she decided to escape to Amsterdam, Holland, and live there. Her

Joking Around with Batwing Lubricant

Actor and comedian Robin Williams began his career performing stand-up comedy in the clubs in San Francisco.

drug use was getting even more out of hand. Her parents were embarrassed. Margaret said, "My parents lied and told their friends that I was living in the [SOTA] dorms, when in reality I was frying my brains out on LSD in Amsterdam. I came home in a black mood, drug weary and confused about what to do with my life."[4]

Margaret reminded herself that the one thing she knew she was good at was comedy. She became determined to quit drug use and have fun entertaining people. She took a job working in her parents' bookstore in the daytime. In the evening and night she started to hang around comedy clubs again.

Comedy Clubs

There are many different types of nightclubs, places people go in the evening to have fun. Some offer live music for listening or dancing. Others are just for comedians. Among the first were improvisational clubs, where comedians make up routines at the moment instead of scripting them in advance. The earliest opened in big cities in the late 1950s and early 1960s. Some of the most famous are The Improv and The Comedy Store in Los Angeles, Second City in Chicago, and Carolines on Broadway in New York City. Some of today's most famous comedians and comedy actors began their careers at comedy clubs. These include Chris Rock, Dave Chapelle, Adam Sandler, Tina Fey, and Amy Poehler.

Joking Around with Batwing Lubricant

In time, club managers got to know Margaret and offered her opportunities to perform for an audience. It was the first step of Margaret's dream of becoming a professional comedian. One club where Margaret often performed was the Rose and Thistle. It was very convenient for her to get to. The Rose and Thistle was located on the floor above her parents' bookstore.

Even though she now had chances to make an audience laugh, being able to do it was another thing. Margaret would be nervous all day long thinking about her performance that evening. She wondered if she might forget her jokes onstage. Or maybe nobody would laugh. What if hardly anyone showed up? Maybe the audience would be filled with people who were drunk and hostile. What if she had to go onstage right after a comedian who had the audience in stitches—would she be a letdown?

Her worries only got worse while she was waiting for her turn to entertain. In the few minutes between the time her name was announced and she told her opening joke, Margaret would break into cold sweats. Her hands shook as it seemed to take forever to walk to the stage.

There were even occasions when she felt like bolting out of the club. But she always stayed. Usually, her nervousness would go away after she told her first joke. But while many of her performances went just fine, there were times when she knew she just wasn't funny. She tackled those poorly received nights like someone who fell off a bicycle. The key was to get back on the bike right away. For Margaret, it was to do another performance as soon as possible. If the next performance went well, she regained her confidence.

Sweetriver Saloons and *Star Search*

By the late 1980s, Margaret was becoming known as an up-and-coming San Francisco-area comedian. A restaurant named Sweetriver Saloon presented comedians on weekends to entertain its customers. There were several Sweetriver Saloons in northern California. Most were in small cities, San Francisco suburbs, or farming towns.

Famous comedians travel by airplane. Some have private jets. The most successful are driven by professional chauffeurs in limousines. Margaret was a beginner and did not have those luxuries. On weekends, she drove her own car usually by herself to her home gigs. Because she did not have much money, she often stayed in dirty or run-down motels.

As is typical with all entertainers, she had both good and bad performances. Sometimes it depended on the audience. An audience could consist of people who simply didn't like her style of humor. As before, there were times when people were drunk and didn't pay attention. But there were plenty of successful nights, and Margaret felt good making people laugh.

Because she was becoming better known, Margaret decided to try out for a spot on a reality talent contest television show called *Star Search*. *Star Search* was open for anyone, but the show's producers decided to try a

Joking Around with Batwing Lubricant

For Cho, performing a stand-up routine onstage was terrifying, but it was also exhilirating and addictive.

Margaret Cho: Comedian, Actress, and Activist

Star Search

Star Search was a big, splashy talent show that ran on television from 1983 through 1995. The staff at *Star Search* looked for talented people in varied fields of entertainment. Those included singing, acting, dancing, and joke-telling. A panel of producers and agents judged the performances and the winner returned the next week to face new competition. Some of the amateur talents who appeared on *Star Search* and went on to success in show business include Chris Rock, Rosie O'Donnell, Britney Spears, Christina Aguilera, and Destiny's Child including Beyoncé. Many who didn't become famous went on to have minor success. Some observers said that nine out of ten *Star Search* contestants found at least jobs in the entertainment business.[5]

version for foreign contestants only. It was called *Star Search International*.

Cho was selected to try out for *Star Search International*. That was despite the fact that it was supposed to be for contestants from other countries. It was clear that Cho was not chosen for the more successful *Star Search* purely because of her race. Although she didn't win, she said the bigger disappointment was not being asked to appear on the original *Star Search*. In fact, on one occasion a *Star Search International* staff member whose job was to help improve the talent asked Cho to try to appear more Chinese. Of course, being Korean-American Cho couldn't help but feel that comment was an insult.

36

Joking Around with Batwing Lubricant

Cho competed on the international version of the popular talent show *Star Search*. Though she didn't win, she did gain exposure.

Chapter 4

All-American Girl

It was painful to Cho that some saw her as a Korean girl before they saw her as a comedian. Comedians are used to getting heckled, or teased, by audience members during live performances. They will loudly insult performers who they don't find entertaining. Rude as those comments can be, professional performers get used to them. In fact, the best comedians find a way to insult the hecklers in return. Much of the time, the comedians' comebacks are better than the hecklers' original comments.

In Cho's case, the heckling she took was almost always race related. Hecklers made fun of her facial features, such as her eyes. They shouted negative remarks about Korean culture. One of the most common comments compared her to the classic movie monster, Godzilla (despite the fact that Godzilla took place in Japan, not Korea). Margaret had by now polished her act and was comfortable onstage. She was a natural at tossing out comeback lines that put hecklers in their places.

Brutal comments weren't limited to audience members. Directors and casting agents, people who help directors decide who to hire to be in a television show, movie, or play, can be cruelly honest. On one occasion she went to an audition, or tryout, for a role in a science fiction movie. In auditions, actors usually read lines from a script. The casting director was not happy with Cho's reading. After Cho had finished, the casting director barked at her. He told her to take acting classes.

Many times a casting agent's criticisms can be right on target. In that case, the actor should try to improve. Sometimes acting classes help. Then again, perhaps the casting agent was wrong. Actors need the ability to look at themselves honestly.

A Bright Future in Show Business

Margaret kept trying. As she did at Sweetriver Saloon restaurants, Margaret began doing shows at a variety of venues. These included college campuses, clubs, theaters, and shopping malls. So Cho went back to a life of long hours driving, entertaining people in the evening, and staying overnight in low-cost motels. That lifestyle got

Margaret Cho: Comedian, Actress, and Activist

tiresome. But it provided Margaret with both money and work experience.

Cho got an agent named Karen. The job of an agent is to help a performer get gigs. Many performers are good entertainers, but not good at knowing how much they should be paid. So the agent negotiates with a club owner or television or movie production company owner. Together they arrive at a fair payment for the entertainer.

Not many entertainers can truly succeed without a good agent. Hiring Karen was a big move in Cho's career. In Margaret, Karen saw a woman who was tremendously talented. Karen firmly believed that with her guidance Margaret had a bright future in show business. But Margaret still had trouble with confidence. Cho wrote, "I was suspicious of her. I could not believe that anyone would be so interested in me just for my talent."[1]

Her hard work began to pay off. Word started to get out on college and university campuses all over the country about this funny and talented Asian-American female comedian. Before long, Margaret Cho was in demand. Her life underwent a huge change almost immediately. At one point she performed over three hundred concerts over the course of just two years.[2]

Now that she had made a name for herself, Margaret was signed to appear on a few television shows. She was not the star on any. In fact, most of her appearances were brief. One was a guest role in a sitcom titled *The Golden Palace*, about four elderly women running a small hotel

All-American Girl

As Cho's star began to rise, she was booked on Arsenio Hall's wildly popular nighttime talk show.

Margaret Cho: Comedian, Actress, and Activist

in Florida. She also got a role doing the voice of a cartoon character in an animated series called *The Critic*. Most importantly, she was booked, or hired, to do stand-up comedy on a nighttime talk show called *The Arsenio Hall Show*. While similar shows at the time drew audiences mostly of middle-aged or older people, Hall was edgier than the other hosts. So Margaret, in her early twenties, and her style of humor would fit in perfectly with Hall's viewers.

She also made a television appearance on a special hosted by Bob Hope.

Bob Hope

Bob Hope was a legendary comedian and actor. At his peak, he was one of the most famous people in the world. He had his first big successes making movies in the 1930s. When television started to become popular in the 1950s, Hope easily made the tradition from the big screen to the small screen.

For many years Hope hosted the annual Academy Awards, also known as the Oscars. People loved Hope for taking entertainers overseas to perform for American military people serving in far away wars. On several occasions he risked his life doing those shows. They were regularly videotaped and aired in the United States as one-time only special television presentations. Hope did numerous other comedy television specials, too.

Cho was booked to appear on one of Hope's specials. At first it seemed like a mismatch. By that time Hope was pushing ninety years of age. It might seem that a Bob Hope special would be the last place for an edgy comedian like Cho. Unlike Cho's political views, Hope's views were conservative. But this special was titled *Bob Hope Presents the Ladies of Laughter*. Other than Hope, it featured only women comedians.

Hope was so famous and had such a large following that she happily accepted the gig. Television audiences knew that if the legendary Bob Hope wanted her to appear on one of his specials, she must be good. It aired the Saturday after Thanksgiving in 1992.

Cho's agent, Karen, was continuing to do her job well. At her request, Cho hired a business manager named Greer. Karen and Greer together were getting Margaret ready for her next career move. With the exposure she was getting from her television appearances, they felt it was time for Margaret to star in her own sitcom. All those long days traveling from one low-paying gig to another seemed to now be worth it.

Ready for Prime Time?

All-American Girl was a sitcom that was a dream project for Margaret. The show's producers, however, wanted to tone down the antics of the character Margaret was to play. They didn't want Margaret to be too rebellious because they were hoping the show would air at 8 p.m. At that time a lot of young children are watching television. The producers stressed that Cho's show should be one

Margaret Cho: Comedian, Actress, and Activist

In 1992, Cho landed a coveted spot on a Bob Hope comedy special. Hope was a legendary performer known for entertaining US troops.

where parents and children could feel comfortable watching it together. Although Margaret had dealt with severe drug problems in her life, controversial subjects like that would not be discussed.

The creative people at ABC fleshed out the plot. Margaret's mother, Katherine Kim, played by Jodi Long, was the stricter parent. She wanted Margaret only to date successful Korean men. She was concerned that Margaret might become too American and lose her Korean heritage. Her father, Benny Kim, was played by Clyde Kusatsu. Benny was a firm father, but not as traditional as her mother. He spent much of his time at home trying to be the peacemaker during Margaret and Katherine's many arguments. Like Margaret Cho's real-life parents, Margaret Kim's parents in *All-American Girl* owned a bookstore.

There were several other regular characters on the show. Stuart, played by B. D. Wong, was Margaret's serious older brother. While Margaret was rebellious, Stuart was nerdy and obedient. Margaret liked to go on dates while Stuart preferred to stay home and study. Her twelve-year-old brother Eric was played by J. B. Quon. Eric idolized Margaret, which didn't sit well with their mother. Rounding out the Kim home was Grandma, played by Amy Hill. She was always making outrageous or strange statements. Some of the things she said may have sounded crazy. But if one thought deeply about her comments, they made sense.

Margaret Cho: Comedian, Actress, and Activist

Cho stands with her TV family in a promotional photo for *All-American Girl*, the sitcom built around her that promised to be her big break.

Outside the home, Margaret worked in the cosmetics section of a department store. One of her two coworkers was Ruthie, played by Maddie Corman. The other was Gloria, played by Judy Gold. Neither was Asian. Ruthie and Gloria were among Margaret's best friends. They encouraged Margaret to keep up her active and rebellious lifestyle.

Just two weeks before the pilot was videotaped, Margaret was called to the studio to do a screen test. A screen test is similar to an audition. Margaret stood in front of a camera and read words written for her character to say. But in an audition, actors are trying out for a part. The purpose of the screen test was to see how Margaret looked on television.

Soon after doing the screen test Margaret received a call from the show's head producer, a woman named Gail. Gail told Margaret over the phone that there was a problem. Important people at ABC felt she was too heavy to play the lead character. They were especially concerned about her face. They thought it looked too puffy. Cho said, "What hurt most was that it was not a body part I could hide . . . How did I not run and scream when the cameras were in on me, to spare the world a glimpse of this huge face that could barely fit on the screen?"[3]

Gail told Margaret that she would have to lose weight to play the part. As soon as Margaret ended the conversation with Gail she spoke to her agent, Karen. Karen suggested that Margaret quit the show. She explained to Margaret that her physical appearance is part of who she is. Her weight is one of the topics Margaret often jokes about in her stand-up routines. By making her lose weight the people at the network were trying to turn Margaret into something she wasn't.

But Margaret knew quitting the show would set her career backwards. She would have go back to performing at clubs and colleges all over the country. That would mean a return to long hours of driving and more nights in cheap motels. She didn't want to return to that lifestyle. Margaret decided she would go on a crash diet and do the show.

Karen didn't let up. She kept telling Margaret that it was not in her best interest to lose weight to pretend to be something she is not. But Margaret disagreed with her. She fired Karen and got a new agent.

The next two weeks were punishing. In order to lose a substantial amount of weight in such a short time, Margaret went on a strict exercise routine. She hired a personal trainer to get her into shape. For six days a week over the next two weeks the personal trainer came to Margaret's door at 7 a.m. in the morning. He led Margaret in exercises for four hours every day. Working out so strenuously was painful and tiresome.

But the tough part had only begun.

Chapter 5

TOO ASIAN OR NOT ASIAN ENOUGH

Margaret also was ordered to go on a special diet. Over the next two weeks she ate nothing but small portions of low-calorie foods. She went to bed hungry every night and seemed to dream about nothing but food. To feel full, she drank a lot of water day and night.

When the two weeks were up, Margaret had lost thirty pounds. She was now thin enough to play the lead role on her television show. But losing so much weight in such a short time isn't healthy. Medical experts say it is best for a dieter to lose weight gradually.

A Health Scare

Margaret attended rehearsals for the pilot. The actors who would play Margaret's family and friends were hired. None of the Asian actors that were cast as her family members were Korean. Margaret thought that was odd. But as the rehearsals were going on and the cast members were getting to know each other, Margaret started to feel physically sick. She went to the bathroom and as she started to urinate blood came out. Her body was weak and in pain.

She knew this was serious and went right away to a hospital. The medical staff examined Cho and discovered her kidneys had collapsed. It was an effect of her extreme dieting.

Cho was treated and released. In spite of the pain, Margaret became even more obsessed with her weight. She didn't want to put on all the weight she lost. The pilot of her show was ready to be videotaped. If she regained the weight would the network cancel the show? Margaret didn't know but did not want to take any chances.

Margaret told as few people as possible that she had been hospitalized. She feared people would tell her to stop dieting. That would have been for her own well-being. But she believed that she needed to diet to remain thin so she wouldn't lose the show.

Addictive Substances

The constant dieting made Margaret feel as if she had no energy. There was the constant pain she suffered as

Too Asian or Not Asian Enough

Cho began a campaign of dangerous dieting when network executives told her that she wasn't pretty or thin enough.

a result of her weakened kidneys. Still, she was driven to keep her weight down. A doctor prescribed some diet pills for her. While they helped Margaret maintain her weight loss, there were side effects, including severe migraine headaches and panic attacks.

In addition to taking the pills, Margaret experimented with other methods of keeping the weight off. She took several types of laxatives. She also started exercising more and more often, going outdoors on her breaks to run. A female actor told Margaret that she didn't get hungry at night because she drank two small shots of an alcohol called tequila, which made her feel full.

Margaret tried drinking tequila, but she found it impossible to stop at two shots. Alcohol is addictive and Margaret would often drink an entire bottle. She started taking drugs and smoking marijuana to kill some of the side effects of the diet pills. When her doctor stopped prescribing the diet pills, she found a way to get them illegally. Before long she had fallen back into another stretch of drug abuse. Margaret confessed, "I thought if I could be thin, then I could be happy, but it wasn't true. I was thinner than I had ever been and totally miserable."[1]

The Publicity Train

While Cho was struggling with her drug and alcohol issues, the people at ABC accepted her new show. In the few days after the announcement, Margaret lost track of how many interviews she did for entertainment reporters. Professional photographers lined up to take her picture whenever she walked outdoors or into a public area. They called out her name and urged her to move to spots where they could get a better angle of her. Margaret had never been given so much attention.

Over the course of the summer, *All-American Girl* was heavily advertised on ABC television. Advertisements also ran in magazines and newspapers. Margaret appeared on television talk shows urging people to watch *All-American Girl.* Those who were familiar with Cho's style of comedy couldn't wait until the show aired. Korean Americans were just as excited. Even those unfamiliar with Cho's work had heard so much about *All-American Girl* that they were dying to see it.

The Premiere

After much anticipation, *All-American Girl* debuted on television screens across the country on the evening of September 14, 1994. As the show opens, we see the entire Kim family sitting at the dinner table, with one exception: Margaret isn't there. Her father checks his watch and her mother impatiently shakes her head. Little brother Eric wants to start eating, but Katherine says it is Korean tradition that nobody eats until the whole family is at the table.

After a few minutes, Margaret enters the picture. She is talking on a portable phone while walking down the stairs to enter the kitchen. Margaret is dressed like many teenagers did in the 1990s. She is wearing an acid-washed denim jacket and a short dress. She is oblivious to her family. Finally, she realizes that her family is waiting for her before they can start eating.

Margaret Cho: Comedian, Actress, and Activist

Hit Television Shows in 1994

When *All-American Girl* went on the air in 1994 it was a great time for comedians-turned-actors. A total of four of the top ten most watched television programs that year were sitcoms starring people who got their start doing stand-up comedy. These were *Seinfeld* starring Jerry Seinfeld; *Home Improvement* with Tim Allen; *Grace Under Fire* featuring Brett Butler; and *Roseanne* starring Roseanne Barr. A fifth sitcom in the year's top ten was *Friends*. (However, none of the lead actors in *Friends* had been known for doing stand-up comedy.) One other sitcom with a former stand-up comedian in the lead role finished just out of the top ten. It was titled *Ellen*. It starred Ellen DeGeneres, who later went on to host a successful daytime television talk show.[2]

Just after she sits down, an obviously unhappy Katherine says to Margaret, "Do you know why I encourage your brother to become a cardiologist [a doctor whose specialty is to deal with heart problems]? Because I knew some day you'd give me a heart attack." Then she snaps at Margaret, "What are you wearing?!"[3]

Margaret mentions that she has a date with her boyfriend, a young white man naked Kyle. Katherine disapproves of him, mainly because he is not Korean. Thinking her mother would approve of Kyle if she met him, she invites Kyle to dinner at the Kim family home. Throughout the entire episode Katherine tries to set Margaret up with single and successful young Korean men. Katherine is set in her ways. She has no interest in accepting Kyle.

Out of anger and frustration, Margaret makes an announcement that she knows will drive her mother crazy. She blurts out that she is leaving the family home and moving with Kyle into an apartment. Near the end of the episode, Margaret is about to take the big step and leave her house. But just before she walks out the door, Grandma tells Margaret that she has a housewarming gift for her.

Grandma ducks into her bedroom before returning with a beautiful parakeet in a cage. Margaret wants to keep it. But the apartment she plans to move into doesn't accept people with pets. Because she doesn't want to turn down her grandma's gift, Margaret decides to stay home to the delight of her family.

We then learn that Grandma knew all along that the apartment does not accept pets. She knew if she gave the parakeet to Margaret that Margaret wouldn't have the heart to leave home. The audience also gets the feeling that Margaret felt all along that she never really wanted to move out of her home.

A Tepid Reception

The audience that tuned in to watch *All-American Girl* —especially those familiar with Cho's stand-up comedy and especially Korean Americans—was hoping for the best. Instead, many were disappointed. They hoped in time *All-American Girl* would improve as the television season went on.

The plot of the next episodes included one about Grandma meeting a wealthy and handsome older Korean man who asks her to marry him and another about Margaret planning to drop out of college to manage a rock band.

The professional critics and the viewers had all sorts of complaints. Margaret Cho fans were disappointed that the character Margaret Kim had hardly anything in common with the Margaret Cho they had seen do stand-up. Cho's routines were usually loud, crude, and in-your-face. But whereas Margaret Cho was wild, Margaret Kim was mild. Margaret Kim was rebellious, but in a polite way. Her personality was toned down from Cho's.

The fact that the show was aired during family time certainly had a lot to do with it. While there is nothing wrong with polite rebellion, in this case it was out of character for the star. Among the credits that ran on the television screen as the show had was ending read, "Based on the stand-up comedy of Margaret Cho."[4] In reality, *All-American Girl* had very little to do with Cho's stand-up routines.

Many who knew little about Cho decided to watch *All-American Girl* out of curiosity. It had been promoted and advertised all summer long. But a lot of the viewers just didn't find the show funny or original. The dialogue seemed forced and the plotlines were tired. It seemed like any other sitcom but with an Asian cast.

Too Asian or Not Asian Enough

All-American Girl morphed into something that had very little to do with Margaret Cho or her original comedy.

Julia

All-American Girl was similar to another pioneering sitcom: *Julia*. Julia Baker was an African-American nurse and single mother played by well-known singer Diahann Carroll. It premiered on September 17, 1968. There had been other television programs with African-American characters. But in nearly all of those shows, they were stereotypes such as butlers or maids.

As with *All-American Girl*, *Julia* took a hearty share of criticism. Some said Julia's life wasn't a realistic example of an African-American's life in the United States in 1968. She lived in a nice home in a comfortable middle-class neighborhood. The fact that millions of African Americans were living in poverty in tough neighborhoods was more or less ignored. *Julia*, however, paved the way for many more shows representing all facets of African-American life.

The Korean-American Audience Reacts

Korean Americans were among the biggest critics. One of their biggest complaints was that Cho was the only Korean American in the cast. To them, it continued a stereotype that to white people all Asians—regardless of their countries of origin—look alike. Ellen Thun, a Korean American and film buff said, "They would have had a good show had they spent even a week with a real Korean-American family, instead of creating that hokey make-believe family."[5]

Other Korean Americans, many of Cho's age, were upset about inaccuracies. Some went right to the opening scene of the pilot. A writer named E. Alex Jung objected to the notion that it is a Korean custom not to begin a meal until all family members are seated. Jung explained that no such custom exists in Korean culture. Instead, Korean custom dictates that people don't eat until the eldest member starts.[6]

There were several scenes where Margaret and Katherine got into loud arguments and insulted each other. Critics countered that Korean-American children, even if they are young adults like Margaret, typically do not challenge their parents so aggressively. At times, the Kim family spoke Korean to each other. But Korean Americans said their accents did not sound real. Because Margaret was the only Korean American in the cast, that wasn't surprising. Many also had problems with the set. The furniture and tableware came from many Asian cultures, not just Korean.

If those weren't enough, some observers felt that the main characters reinforced stereotypes. They felt that was especially true of Katherine, whose strictness made her seem like a stereotyped Asian tiger mom. The Asian tiger mom runs her home with a iron fist and strict rules. She has unrealistic expectations for her children. And nerdy Stuart seemed too obedient to be realistic. Overall, most critics thought all the characters (with perhaps the exception of Grandma) were two-dimensional. They were lacking in depth. They seemed more like clichés than real people.

Not everyone disliked *All-American Girl*. On the website International Movie Database (imdb.com), television viewers gave it a quality rating of 6.8 out of a possible 10.[7] Korean-American writer Philip Chung was pleased that television was presenting to the public a warm Korean-American family. They loved each other even if they had their differences. More importantly, it exposed non-Korean television viewers to a Korean-American family.

Margaret felt criticized from all directions. Some viewers felt her character was "too Asian." On the other hand, there were people who said she was "not Asian enough." She commented, "The weirdness of being the first Asian-American—I guess, for lack of a better word—star, is that people are constantly judging you."[8]

In a way, people wanted her to represent all Korean Americans. Yet she could not do so because there is no such thing as a typical Korean American any more than there is a typical African American or Irish American. She knew that no matter what she did or how she acted she would not be able to satisfy everyone.

Cho received support from other cast members. Amy Hill, who played Grandma, told Cho, "After watching what you went through, it made me think I don't ever want to be the star of any show."[9]

Still, because *All-American Girl* was the first sitcom to feature a mostly all-Asian cast, it was a groundbreaking moment on television.

Chapter 6

"THIS ISN'T ME. THIS IS STUPID."

Due to *All-American Girl*'s low ratings, the producers made some changes. They decided to try letting Margaret Kim be more independent. When viewers turned on their televisions to watch the fourteenth episode on the evening of January 11, 1995, the first thing they saw was Margaret telling her parents she wanted to move into her own place.

Because she doesn't have the money to pay for her own apartment, Margaret rents an apartment with her coworkers Ruthie and Gloria. At first everything is fine. In time, though, the three are fighting like cats and dogs. So Margaret moves back home.

In the last scene, Margaret and her mother are in the basement of their home doing laundry. Margaret complains that she will never find a decent apartment that she can afford. Katherine gets an idea. How about if Margaret moved into the family's basement? She tries to tell Margaret, but Margaret is too busy feeling sorry for herself to listen.

As Margaret is walking away, she hits her head on a lit lightbulb hanging from the ceiling. For a moment, she stands silently with the lightbulb just over her head. It looks just like a comic strip scene where a character gets a great idea and the idea is represented by a lightbulb. Margaret announces, "Hey, wait a minute. I could move into the basement." Katherine responds sarcastically, "The basement. Very smart. You should work for NASA (National Aeronautics and Space Administration)."[1]

In the new next episode, Margaret is living in her new basement apartment ready to embark on a new life of independence. But this fresh start in the story line made little difference to television viewers. The ratings continued to sag.

So the producers tried an even bigger change. They shot another episode to be broadcast on March 15, 1995. In this one, Margaret has moved out of her house and is renting an apartment with three men. Except for Grandma, Margaret's entire family has been written out of the show.

The show's regular viewers found the new episode confusing. Used to seeing Margaret interacting with her family, they were stunned to discover several new characters. It appeared that this new version of the show wasn't going to work either. ABC chose not to make any

"This Isn't Me. This Is Stupid."

more episodes. Margaret had no choice but to face the unfortunate truth. *All-American Girl* was canceled, or taken off the air.

In the following months, Cho tried analyzing why *All-American Girl* didn't catch on. One time, she confessed, "The comedy on the show was very bland and very middle of the road, it was a great disappointment to a lot of people."[2] On another occasion, she said, "I thought it was really too much of a kids' show, and it wasn't really what I did as a stand-up comedian. They had understood me as a performer wrongly."[3]

A Downward Spiral

Margaret went back to playing comedy clubs but with no specific goal in mind. She went from gig to gig, taking time out to make another short trip to Europe. Much of the time she hung around with friends at her home in Los Angeles. Without any specific aims in her life, Margaret found herself back into her old routines of loafing, drinking, doing drugs, and chain-smoking cigarettes.

On more than one occasion she was under the influence of mind-altering substances when she went onstage to perform. In a show in Monroe, Louisiana, Margaret was so drunk she couldn't perform well. The audience was filled with eight hundred students who had paid to see what they hoped would be a funny show. The audience got angry; what they saw was a waste of their money. They booed her continuously. Margaret walked off the stage in defeat.[4] She remembered about

Margaret Cho: Comedian, Actress, and Activist

those days, "Sometimes I would have to hang onto the microphone to keep the room from spinning."[5]

It was just a matter of time before Margaret's vices would affect her health. One morning she woke in bed and tried to speak. She had totally lost her voice. She rushed to a doctor's office where she was given a medical test. A tiny camera was lowered into her throat to take pictures of her vocal chords. The results showed that they were covered with white dots.

The doctor gave her strict orders. One was to quit smoking cigarettes. The other was to stop smoking marijuana. At first Margaret found a way to keep using marijuana while not smoking it. She ate food that had pot cooked into it. That mainly consisted of dessert items. As time went on she did it more and more often. But at one point she realized enough was enough. She wrote, "Then, as I crammed more and more psychedelic sweets into my mouth, thinking more meant more heaven, it was just disgusting."[6]

Around this time, she also went through a tough breakup with a boyfriend. While the doctor had given Margaret strict orders to quit tobacco and marijuana, he didn't mention alcohol. She abused alcohol to dull the pain of her breakup.

Because Margaret is a creative person she decided to put her feelings in writing. Margaret began writing a screenplay about her failed romance. She hoped to sell it to a studio that would make it into a movie. At the same

"This Isn't Me. This Is Stupid."

time, Margaret hoped that being so busy working on a screenplay could take her attention away from alcohol.

Most writers take weeks or even months to write a first draft of a screenplay. Margaret was so excited about the project that she kept writing and writing and writing. She had a first draft finished in a matter of hours.

Margaret rewrote the script a few more times. She found a film production company that appeared interested in it. The head of the company told Margaret he strongly felt the screenplay had great potential. In time, however, she realized that the man was more interested in her than her screenplay. He made sexual advances toward her. She had no interest in him and reported him to a studio employee. In response, he told Margaret that her screenplay wasn't good enough to be made into a movie.

Margaret was at one of the lowest points in her career. She found a boyfriend named Marcel, but she continued abusing alcohol. In addition, she was fiercely overeating. Again, Margaret reached a point where she was sick of going to bed drunk and feeling miserable the next day. She made up her mind to change her life once more.

Marcel decided the best way he could help Margaret was to remove all the alcohol from their apartment. He poured all the contents of every bottle they owned down the kitchen sink. Margaret went through a tough time breaking free from her addictions—both to food and alcohol. As she thought over her bad habits, she said, "This isn't me. This is stupid."[7]

Margaret Cho: Comedian, Actress, and Activist

Margaret returned to clubs with a new attitude and healthy lifestyle. She discovered a major change in her performances. "I found a new sense of enthusiasm in my work. Audiences found me funnier, more alive, happy. Sometimes I had drunk because I thought I hated my job. I realized then that I loved my job, and that being [messed] up all the time made me hate it because I couldn't do it properly."[8]

Back on the Road

Marcel and Margaret eventually broke up. Margaret knew it was time to move on with her life. She got together with her old agent, Karen. Karen still had the utmost confidence in Margaret's talent. She booked Margaret for shows at comedy clubs and colleges. By now Margaret no longer had to stay in dingy motels. She was earning a lot of money for her performances.

Sometimes Margaret performed alone. Other times she performed with a comedian named Karen Kilgariff. In between all their touring, Cho and Kilgariff wrote their own sketch comedy show they did regularly at a club in southern California. Cho and Kilgariff's act was titled "The People Tree."

In the show, the two comics depicted a variety of characters doing funny monologues. Margaret based some of the characters on her own life experiences. In one she was an overweight woman unhappy with herself. In another she played a self-absorbed craftswoman.

For quite a while Cho didn't talk about *All-American Girl*. She didn't want to be the kind of person who

"This Isn't Me. This Is Stupid."

Cho often teamed up with fellow comedian Karen Kilgariff, shown above in a 2015 stand-up performance.

constantly complained about her life. However, the longer that she didn't talk about it the more it bothered her. She said, "Being silent for so long had rotted my insides, but when I began to speak, all the misery and despair dissolved."[9]

Cho also realized that if she looked at the experience in a different way, it could seem very humorous. She began to makes jokes about the television show in her performances. It takes a skilled comedian to talk about something bad without sounding like she is feeling sorry for herself. Along the same line, she found a way to discuss the sitcom and all its problems without being depressing. She also discussed her weight and her drug and alcohol use in a humorous manner; very little was off-limits. She mocked stereotypes of Asian women as meek and cracked jokes about the women in her family.

One last topic she put into her show was her relationship with the lesbian, gay, bisexual, and transgender (LGBT) community. She came out publicly as bisexual and talked about her relationship with gay men. As people who were seen as outsiders, she and gay men had that in common. Cho was accepted as a friend by the community and was invited to dance on a float at a gay pride parade.

Margaret has the talent to keep her performances entertaining, regardless of the subject matter. By discussing *All-American Girl* and her life after it was canceled, she let her fans know why she had been out of the spotlight for a while.

"This Isn't Me. This Is Stupid."

Cho actively supported the LGBT community long before it was fashionable. Here, she is shown taking part in the 38th Annual San Francisco LGBT Pride Celebration and Parade in 2008.

I'm the One That I Want

Cho's new material was going over very well with audiences. She started to think about turning that part of her act into a whole new show. She called it "I'm the One That I Want," based on the famous song that closes the movie *Grease*, "You're the One That I Want." She decided to premier her new show in New York City. In June 1999, she performed "I'm the One That I Want" for the first time at the Westbeth Theatre Center.

Anyone in the audience expecting Cho to act like her character in *All-American Girl* was in for a shock. But those who knew her through her nightclub routines were thrilled. On stage she was once more the gritty,

Margaret Cho: Comedian, Actress, and Activist

> ## Westbeth
>
> Westbeth is an unusual concept. It is officially called Westbeth Artists Housing. It consists of several old buildings that have been transformed into a place for people in the arts to live and work. Most of the buildings were part of Bell Telephone Laboratories from 1898 through 1966. It is appropriate that several actors live here because the earliest experimental versions of television were developed in these buildings in 1929. Westbeth is named for two of the streets that border the complex: West and Bethune.

foul-mouthed, judgmental comedian she had been before she tackled television. Her material consisted of controversial topics: these included racism as well as her addictions to alcohol, diet pills, and other drugs. Much of the time onstage she talked freely about her sex life. She joked about funny experiences on a lesbian cruise.

Cho was pleased to tell her audiences about her acceptance by and friendships with gay men. She frequently peppered her monologue with the word "faggot." While a lot of people find that word demeaning and offensive, Margaret got away with it for one major reason: she identified with the gay community. It was as if they were part of her family. She wasn't an outsider using the term as an insult; she was trying to reclaim it.

She told audiences why, in her view, the sitcom didn't work. "It was supposed to be a family show. I was supposed to be young and cute. It really turned out to be like, Saved by the Gong."[10] (That was a lighthearted reference to a late 1990s sitcom, *Saved by the Bell*. It took place in a high school. The show did have episodes on controversial topics, but it was very family friendly.)

She also discussed her issues with weight. Cho recalled, "I got a phone call that night from the producer of the show, a woman named Gail—someone who I had come to love and trust. She said, 'There's a problem. The network is concerned about the fullness of your face. They think you are really overweight.' I didn't know what to say to that. I always thought I was okay-looking." Cho then shifted her delivery from everyday talk into a robust scream. "I had no idea that I was this giant face taking over America."[11]

Margaret Cho performed during the 16th Annual Gay and Lesbian Alliance Against Defamation (GLAAD) Media Awards at the Kodak Theater on April 30, 2005, in Hollywood, California.

Margaret also shared some tender moments from that period in her life. She remembered the time an executive called her to tell her *All-American Girl* was going to be made into a series. "It was for the first time in my life . . ." Then she paused and slowly but deliberately said the word "acceptance." "I had never found acceptance anywhere—not from my family, not from kids on the playground, not from high school, certainly not from other stand-up comedians. I had never found acceptance until that moment. I felt real. I felt alive. I felt for the first time in my life that I was not invisible."[12]

Chapter 7

LINING UP AROUND THE BLOCK

As much as it is cool to be famous and be recognized by strangers, fame also has a dark side. Margaret included that in her show, too. She laughed as she discussed lies told about her in tabloid newspapers. Tabloid newspapers are often found on stands by the cashiers in supermarkets. The topics are almost always gossip about famous people. Most of the gossip consists of bad things about celebrities. And much of it is made up.

Cho announced that she opened up a tabloid one day and saw the words, "Margaret Cho has thunder thighs." As much as she didn't want to let those words hurt her, she couldn't help it. She was trying so hard to lose weight. She joked, "I would open up a tabloid, see the

Chowlike Cho diet, which was this fake diet that I never went on, with all these fake quotes from me like, 'When I was young I was raised on rice and fish. So when I get heavy I go back to that natural Asian way of eating.'"[1] Margaret kidded that the article made her sound more like the Disney character Mulan than herself.

"I'm the One That I Want" was a smash. Cho's performances sold out nightly. She kept audiences riveted and not just because her jokes are funny. She performed with excellent timing, pausing at the right moment to keep her audiences anticipating what she will say next. After many performances in New York City she took the show to different cities in the United States and elsewhere. In 1999 she performed it in Europe. She was as loved overseas as much as she was at home. Critic Leo Benedictus in the prestigious *London Guardian* daily newspaper raved, "Cho's style, which mixes silly voices with crude but uncontroversial observational gags, is superbly polished. She also has a special wit about her."[2]

He added, "What really sets the show apart, however, is Cho's straightforwardness about her past . . . Instead of killing the mood, these revelations fuel laughter by showing how much all this really means to her." He concluded his review by gushing, "Cho is funny, absolutely, but in its unvarnished honesty this show also feels like a privilege to watch."[3]

A performance Cho did in her hometown of San Francisco was filmed and released as a roughly ninety-minute-long feature movie in 2000. Most audiences and professional critics liked the movie. Dennis Harvey is a critic for *Variety*, a publication written for people in the entertainment business. Harvey thought the movie was a laugh-out-loud riot. He cautioned that people who don't like dirty and raunchy humor would probably be offended. But that seemed to be what he felt made it just fine for the kind of audience that loved that kind of humor. Harvey called the movie, "gleefully tasteless." He added, "What really dominates [the] performance is Cho's crude, rude, ribald humor."[4]

Reviews aside, the movie version of "I'm the One That I Want" was a financial success. It earned over $1.2 million.[5] She then used much of the material from "I'm the One That I Want" to write a short autobiography. She told an interviewer named Greg Herren from the *Lambda Book Report* publication, "I always wanted to write a book. I mean, I grew up with books, and reading is such a wonderful way to connect with an author, don't you think?"[6]

Notorious C.H.O.

On the heels of "I'm the One That I Want," Margaret premiered a new live show in 2001. It was titled "Notorious C.H.O." The title was a parody on the name of a rapper who went by the name "The Notorious B.I.G." Why did she choose that name for her show? Margaret explained, "It was such a captivating thing to call myself notorious." She then laughed, "I had enough letters in my last name [for it] to make sense."[7]

Margaret Cho: Comedian, Actress, and Activist

Cho channeled her disappointment over the cancellation of her show into a one-woman show (and book) called *I'm the One That I Want*.

Her "Notorious C.H.O." show was a blockbuster. Cho did her act in thirty-seven cities across the United States including one in New York City's renowned Carnegie Hall. Because many Asian Americans have excelled at classical music, Margaret offered a joke to her audience that would have worked in few other places. She said, "I'm pretty sure I'm the first Korean-American woman who has ever stood on this stage without a violin."[8]

Like "I'm the One That I Want," "Notorious C.H.O." was made into a movie. And like "I'm the One That I Want," "Notorious C.H.O." was not for people who are easily offended or socially conservative.

The movie *Notorious C.H.O.* was filmed at a performance in Seattle, Washington, on a rainy January day in 2002. It isn't until about six minutes into the movie that Cho's comedy performance actually starts. Some of the things we see in the first six minutes are scenes

Carnegie Hall

Carnegie Hall in New York City is a showplace where only the best of the best are called to perform. For many years, Carnegie Hall was home only to classical music. But in the 1930s and 1940s some of the most talented jazz musicians gave concerts there. And in the 1960s and 1970s classic rock acts such as the Beatles, the Rolling Stones, Led Zeppelin, and the Beach Boys performed on the Carnegie Hall stage. For Margaret, being booked to play Carnegie Hall was a special honor.

of her fans going to the theater and repeating some of their favorite lines from *I'm the One That I Want*. Quite a few fans are from the Asian and LGBT communities. Interspersed with those scenes are several shots of Cho making comments directly to the camera. She comes off as very sweet and welcoming.

At one point, she expresses her appreciation for her followers and at the same time addresses her insecurity. "I'm so excited that there are fans lining up around the block and they are coming to see me, and I hope that I can always deliver."[9]

Also included in the first six minutes are interview segments with Margaret's parents. In one segment Margaret says it feels "surreal" having her parents in the audience. But her parents seem OK with it. In fact, Margaret's mother says that when she was in the women's bathroom she went up to people and said, "Thank you very much for coming to see my daughter." The film then cuts to a clip of Margaret laughing and saying, "I can't believe my mother was in the bathroom thanking people. That is so her, though. She is so gracious about the whole thing."[10]

Wearing a blue plaid shirt and jeans in the movie, Cho jokes about everything including a recent visit to Scotland, her gay male friends, intimate medical procedures, and of course, growing up as an Asian American. At one point, Cho tells the audience, "I have been a comic for a long time. I have always wanted to do this since I was a kid. But I never saw Asian people on television or in movies." She then changes her tone of voice to sound like a preteen confessing her ultimate dream. "Maybe some day," Cho says, "I can be an extra on M*A*S*H."[11]

Cho excels at doing a wide range of voices onstage. She makes expressions as if her face is made of rubber. Depending on the subject of the joke, she can do the voice of a tough man or a little girl. But one voice she is especially known for is that of her mother. She talks about the time her mother was on vacation in Israel and accidentally fell off a camel she was riding. Thankfully, she wasn't severely injured. But Margaret thought her mother's first words after falling were funny and very typical of her mother. Onstage Margaret scrunches up

M*A*S*H

M*A*S*H was a hugely popular sitcom that aired on television from 1972 through 1983. It was about a group of Army doctors and nurses serving in the Korean War in the early 1950s. The acronym, MASH, stood for mobile army surgical hospital. Even though M*A*S*H was a comedy, it was controversial at times for the realistic way it depicted war. People were injured and died in the show, as is the case in real war. In one famous bittersweet episode, a beloved doctor is finished with his Army duties and ready to fly home to his family in the United States. However, he dies when the airplane he is flying in crashes. Many viewers were outraged by that. But M*A*S*H was very thought provoking.

her face and in a thick Korean accent says, "How can this happen to Mommy? I am such a nice person."[12] Margaret's mother finds herself laughing at her daughter's imitation of her. In the movie, she admits, "She [Margaret] does a good impression of me."[13]

Cho addresses personal troubling issues with both compassion and humor. Cho is still very open about her weight issues. When she lets loose about seemingly being on an ongoing diet for much of her life, certainly much of the audience can relate. She discusses the pressure she felt trying to be thin.

She recalls that when she was around ten, "My father made me watch beauty pageants. I could stay up way past my bedtime so I could see what women were supposed to look like. When I lost weight he was so happy, and when I gained weight I became invisible to him. And it taught me that if you are thin, then you are lovable. And I just wanted to be loved."[14]

She goes on to poke fun at her failure to be thin. She admits to herself that perhaps her build is naturally heavyset. She tells herself not to struggle with things she can't change. She would diet all day, then pig out in the evening. "I would go home and inhale everything in the refrigerator—cake, spaghetti, hot dogs, mayonnaise. I ate my best friend." Then she says in the squeaky voice of a ten-year-old girl, "Hey, guys, don't be mad. I totally ate Carla," as laughter resounds through the theater.[15]

Most critics loved her movie. David Noh of the website filmjournal.com raved, "Margaret Cho asserts

Lining Up Around the Block

One of Cho's most famous—and most successful—bits is when she imitates her mother.

MARGARET CHO: COMEDIAN, ACTRESS, AND ACTIVIST

Although she is the butt of many of her daughter's jokes, Margaret Cho's mother can't help but laugh along. She is her daughter's biggest fan, despite once being very critical of her.

her eminence as the funniest woman alive with her second performance film, *Notorious Cho*."[16] Another critic, Jeff Vice, also praised the film. Interestingly, Vice writes movie reviews for the *Deseret News*, a conservative newspaper owned by the Mormon church. It is one of the two main daily newspapers in Salt Lake City, Utah. Vice reported that the movie is "frequently laugh-out-loud funny." He added that "Cho's observations about personal self-image are extremely insightful." But he also warned that "much of the material is extremely raunchy, especially the frank language and explicit discussion of both sexual relationships and drug usage."[17]

Chapter 8

"I GOT SQUID AND PEANUTS"

Outside of work Margaret has a busy social life. She has dated both men and women. At one time she was seeing the famous movie director Quentin Tarantino. Some of his award-winning films include *Pulp Fiction* and *Django Unchained*. One of her other boyfriends was rock singer and actor Chris Isaak.

Around 2003 she began seeing another man from the entertainment business. He was not as well known as Tarantino and Isaak. His name is Al Ridenour, and he is a performance artist. On June 13, 2003, Margaret and Al were married in Los Angeles.

The couple did not have a glamorous celebrity lifestyle. They weren't seen at a lot of lavish parties. In fact, they were rarely seen together in public at all.[1] They also had a very untraditional marriage. For one thing, she is bisexual and he is straight. For another, both openly said despite the fact that they were a married couple they were going to see other people.

That kind of marriage is often referred to as an "open marriage." Margaret explained, "We have a really big house. It's kind of like if we wanna have that, it's like 'You can stay on your side or I'll stay on my side.'"[2] Yet Cho insisted their marriage was in an odd way somewhat traditional. She stated, "I'm all about commitment. And I'm all about marriage. And I'm all about family. And I'm queer also." She said that her unusual marriage worked for one main reason: She doesn't get jealous.[3]

Cho married artist Al Ridenour in 2003. Ridenour is associated with the performance troup Art of Bleeding. The two had what Cho described as a conventional marriage.

"I Got Squid and Peanuts"

Revolution

The same year Cho premiered a new comedy show. It was called "Revolution." Like her other shows, "Revolution" was made into a concert movie. This particular show was filmed in Los Angeles. In the late spring of 2004 *Revolution* was first shown at LGBT festivals. It then aired on the Sundance cable television network. *Revolution* was released on DVD in August 2004.

Cho discusses many of the same subjects in *Revolution* as she did in her earlier two films. One different topic she milks for comedy is the administration of President George W. Bush. Being liberal politically, almost all of Cho's personal opinions are the opposite of Bush's. Bush is known for mispronouncing the word *nuclear*. He always seems to pronounce it "nu-cu-ler" instead of "nu-cle-ar." Cho has no problem letting Bush have it for that. In one routine, she imagines what it was like for Bush's Secretary of State Condoleezza Rice to deal with Bush's embarrassing mispronouncing.

Other than that political topic, Cho's movie is filled with the usual crude jokes as well as her memories of being an outsider in school. Taking the stage with her hair in pigtails and wearing a floor-length multilayered dress, she says, "Being from a family of immigrants can be frustrating and embarrassing. You get [strange foods] in your lunch box. All the other kids would get granola bars and Capri Sun. I would get dried fish." She pauses as the audience laughs. Then she adds, "All the other kids got Hohos and Dingdongs. I got squid and peanuts."[4] Another subject she broaches is how few movie roles are offered to Asian actors and actresses. The audience cracks up as she listed parts she has no interest in playing—those that are Asian stereotypes.

"I get offered movie roles all the time," she exclaims. "And I say, 'No, I don't want to play a manicurist.'" As the audience laughs she pantomimes a manicurist trimming a female customer's fingernails. "I don't want to play a really [angry] liquor store owner." She then points her index finger outward as if it is a gun. In some big cities, owners of liquor stores located in tough neighborhoods are Korean American. "I don't want to play an exceptionally good student. I don't want to get off a tour bus and take numerous photographs." A well-known Asian stereotype is being good with technology, especially cameras.[5]

Quite a few critics loved the show, but some complained that it was just more of the same stuff Cho had been doing for years. David Rooney of *Variety* mostly praised Cho's performance. He wrote, "Cho's talent for mimicry is as sharp as ever, though fans may feel cheated that her much-loved impersonation of her mother is featured only in passing here."[6] The Internet critic flickphilosopher.com wasn't as enthusiastic. It says, "There's no question that she's preaching to a particular choir that's urban, liberal, and educated, but even some of the choir will find her sermon tedious."[7]

Regardless, *Revolution* was nominated for a Grammy award in the category of best comedy album. The

"I Got Squid and Peanuts"

Revolution was released in theaters in 2004. Cho's fans loved the show, but critics complained that she was covering familiar territory.

Grammy awards are given annually to the best recorded acts. However, *Revolution* did not win. Weird Al Yankovic did for his comedy album *Poodle Hat*.

Writing Her Way Onto the Silver Screen

Margaret's creative juices were flowing fully. Because she didn't like most of the movie parts offered to her, she decided to write her own film and star in it. It is titled *Bam Bam and Celeste.* Not surprisingly it is about people who don't fit in. Margaret played Celeste, an overweight girl who was into goth-punk as a teenager. Bruce Daniels was cast as her longtime friend, Bam Bam. He is a gay, African-American man. Both Bam Bam and Celeste lived in a Midwestern town. They were each tormented by other kids when they were in school.

Even though they are in their thirties, they still feel like outsiders. Bam Bam and Celeste hear about a reality television show where people considered unattractive are made over to look better. Both Bam Bam and Celeste feel they are exactly what they show is looking for. So they drive to New York City where the program is videotaped.

When they arrive at the television studio they discover that the person in charge of doing makeovers is a former high school classmate who used to bully them. The message of the movie is that true beauty is not based on what a person looks like. True beauty is what one is like inside.

Bam Bam and Celeste was released in 2005. It falls into the category of an adventure comedy. It is a short

"I Got Squid and Peanuts"

Cho wrote and starred in the motion picture *Bam Bam and Celeste*. She posed on the red carpet with costar Katy Selverstone, director Lorene Machado, and costar Bruce Daniels in 2005.

movie, running only an hour and twenty-four minutes. One special touch was that Margaret plays not only Celeste but Celeste's mother, referred to as Mommy. Cho's depiction of Mommy is almost identical to her portrayal of her real mother in her stand-up routines.

Despite Cho's fame, *Bam Bam and Celeste* didn't catch on with moviegoers. It didn't play in many theaters and is almost forgotten today. One reason is likely because the reviews were not very good. The vast majority of fans who rated the movie on Internet Movie Database (imdb.com) found it to be just average, giving it a rating of 5.4 out of ten.[8] Professional critics thought even less of it. Several said it was merely a weaker version of *Romy and*

Michelle's High School Reunion, a movie with a similar plot that came out in 1997.

Ron Gonsalves of filmcritic.com wrote that he has enjoyed Cho's concert films, although sometimes they are too political for his taste. He stated, "Then there's *Bam Bam and Celeste*, which mostly isn't especially political, but also isn't especially funny."[9] He said that except for Celeste, almost every character in the movie is a stereotype.

Gonsalves's observation that Cho seemed to be getting more political was a keen one. Although she continued to do stand-up comedy and take on guest roles on television and in movies, Cho was making more news being a professional activist as well as an entertainer. The public was beginning to see a new side of Margaret Cho.

Chapter 9

THE ACTIVIST

Cho's activism became clear in 2005 when she wrote a book titled *I Have Chosen to Stay and Fight*. In the book, Cho advocates civil liberties such as freedom of speech. She further discusses traditional liberal issues such as feminism, racism, and a strong dislike for President George W. Bush. Much of her prose is very cleverly written. But as usual, she fills the book with vulgarity. That type of language could disturb readers who might otherwise support her views. However, she makes it clear where she stands on the issues.

She writes the following about conservative political commentator Ann Coulter: "As well as betraying her gender, as a notoriously antifeminist woman hater, she is also racist, homophobic, without compassion, inhumane, arrogant, dishonest, contradictory, not funny, has an arguing technique that compares closely to 'I know you are but what am I?,' wears red leather miniskirts and is just plain . . . wrong."[1]

She says of President George W. Bush, "Bush is a liar and a thief, and uses God's name like they grew up together in the 'hood, like they got thug love."[2] That said, Cho takes on some issues with viewpoints that are hard to disagree with. She criticizes the pressure on women to be super thin and she discusses the pain of people who have AIDS (Acquired Immune Deficiency Syndrome).

Of course, a book with strong opinions is bound to be controversial. She tells her readers what women and racial minorities can do to make the world better. Yet, some readers found it offensive that she blames some groups in general for what is wrong with the world. In attacking other people's prejudices, Cho seems to show she has some of her own.

On September 11, 2001, a group of radical Muslims took control of four commercial airliners in the United States. Their goal was to crash them into important buildings. In doing so they killed nearly three thousand innocent people. In *I Have Chosen to Stay and Fight*, Cho criticizes the news coverage of the event. She says there was not enough diversity among the reporters or the people the reporters interviewed.

She writes, "All I ever saw after September 11 was old white man after old white man on [the television news network] CNN talking about what happened."[3] She adds, "No women, no people of color, except for a precious few Muslim and Arab Americans talking about

THE ACTIVIST

this event has [messed] them up because everybody is blaming them just because they have a similar skin color as the perpetrators of this terrible crime."[4]

In reality, numerous women and persons of color covered the attacks. In addition, the secretary of state at the time, Colin Powell, is an African-American man. Bush's staff member, Condoleezza Rice, is an African-American woman. Both appeared on television many times in the wake of the terrorist attack.

Saving Tookie

At the same time *I Have Chosen to Stay and Fight* was published, Cho took part in a public campaign to save

Cho publicly supported the pardoning of death row inmate Stanley Tookie Williams. Many believed the former gang member should be spared the death penalty due to his antigang activism.

a convicted murderer named Stanley Tookie Williams from the death penalty.

It did not matter. Williams was executed in December 2005. In response, Cho wrote in her blog, "I don't know why it surprises me that they executed Tookie last night, but somehow I thought that this was all an elaborate staging for a last minute reprieve. It seemed impossible that they would put him to death, with so much public protest, with so much to say in his defense. If they can kill him, they can kill us all, without reason, without mercy."[5]

She further outraged many when she said onstage during a gala event, "Bush is not Hitler. He would be if he applied himself."[6] As a result many conservatives blasted her and she received a lot of hate mail. People went beyond criticizing her comments. They attacked

Stanley Tookie Williams

Stanley Tookie Williams was for years a feared gang leader in one of the toughest inner-city neighborhoods in Los Angeles. Williams had been convicted of four murders in 1979 and was sentenced to death. But during his twenty-six years in prison, Williams wrote several books with anti-gang and antiviolence messages. Several activists said that Williams was not the same man that he was in the 1970s. They advocated that he was doing a lot of good with his messages. They said Williams should not be set free but should not be put to death. They felt life in prison was a more suitable punishment.

THE ACTIVIST

her weight and her Korean heritage. Cho responded to the meanness with a positive attitude. She wrote, "I actually adore that kind of hate mail, because if all you have to fight me with is prejudice then I've already won the battle, and I'm eventually going to win this war."[7]

True Colors

Cho continued to do her comedy performances and act in both television and the movies. Then in 2007 she took part in something different, the "True Colors" tour. The title refers to a 1986 hit song by Cyndi Lauper. The song's meaning was interpreted by many to be having courage to be true to one's self. In time it became an anthem for the LGBT community.

"True Colors" was organized by Lauper to raise money for LGBT charities. It ran in sixteen cities across the United States in June 2007. The performers were popular musical groups and solo artists, but Cho was the show's host. As host, she introduced the musical acts. It was also up to Cho to keep the audiences entertained between acts.

The respected *New York Times* music section gave the show a stellar review. That included Cho's turn as host. The review read in part, "Margaret Cho, serving comfortably as host, preserved a tone that was breezy, vulgar and knowing."[8]

It wouldn't have been a Cho performance without a few laughs at Asian-American stereotypes. One is that Asians are bad drivers. She announced, "I'm going to get

Margaret Cho: Comedian, Actress, and Activist

Margaret Cho performed as part of the True Colors Festival at the Greek Theater in 2007 in Berkeley, California.

there in my Nissan Sentra, driving 35 miles per hour in the fast lane with my turn signal on the whole time."[9]

Fighting for LGBT Rights

By 2008 Cho was a recognized face in the world of LGBT advocacy. Her hometown, San Francisco, gave her a special honor on April 30. Sometimes towns and cities honor famous people who have achieved positive things with days named in their honor. The honoree doesn't get any special power or privilege. It's a way of letting local heroes know they are appreciated and that their hometowns are proud of them. Who could have thought back when Margaret was an unpopular child constantly getting teased and picked on that the city of San Francisco would in the future declare a "Margaret Cho Day."

In May 2008, the state of California State Supreme Court ruled that same-sex couples in California could be legally married. (It was not yet legal in the entire country.) Almost immediately Cho made an effort to play an active role in this. Within two months she was legally deputized by the city of San Francisco to perform same-sex marriages there. Being deputized meant that Cho was able to preside over a gay marriage and it would be legally accepted.

She told the website eonline.com, "It's a very empowering thing to be able to preside over these ceremonies. We've been working on this for such a long time." She added that her goal was to be legally permitted to perform same-sex marriages in other communities.[10]

Drop Dead Diva

Around this time, Cho decided to take a chance on another television series. The new show was a world apart from *All-American Girl*. It aired on the Lifetime channel, a cable network aimed mostly toward women viewers. Shows on cable networks tend to be a bit more experimental and edgy than those on the commercial networks.

The series was titled *Drop Dead Diva*. While each episode of *All-American Girl* ran for a half hour, *Drop Dead Diva*'s episodes were an hour long. The first episode aired on July 12, 2009. *Drop Dead Diva* was part legal drama, part comedy, and part fantasy. The basic premise was this: An airheaded aspiring model dies in an automobile accident. She returns to Earth in the body of Jane Bingum, a serious but shy, high-powered attorney who had also recently died. At no time can the model tell anyone that she now occupies Jane's body. Cho plays Jane's personal assistant, Terri Lee.

Unlike television programs that feature only thin, glamorous actors, *Drop Dead Diva*'s cast was made up of women of various sizes and shapes. Cho said, "I think it's important because we don't have any images of beautiful, full-figured women. We don't have role models out there that look like real people. If we have more representations of real-looking women on TV, you would have fewer problems with anorexia and bulimia. I think in a lot of ways because of television you have these unnaturally thin ideals of beauty."[11]

The Activist

Cho presided over a symbolic mass gay wedding celebrated by more than one hundred same-sex couples in West Hollywood, California, in 2004.

Margaret Cho: Comedian, Actress, and Activist

As a regular cast member on *Drop Dead Diva*, Cho enjoyed steady employment for five years. The show centered on a plus-sized lawyer whose body was inhabited by the soul of a fashion model.

In 2010, she took a new comedy show on tour. It was called "Cho Dependent." The title was a play on words. A codependent is a person who depends on others to get through the tough parts of life. "Cho Dependent" was a departure for the comic. It was her first album recorded not onstage but in a recording studio. It also included her singing self-written comedy songs as well as traditional joke-telling.

Like all of Cho's work, "Cho Dependent" was not for all tastes. Regardless, it became Cho's second Grammy-nominated comedy album. However, the winner for best comedy album went to Lewis Black's *Stark Raving Black*.

Playing a Korean Dictator

Cho's television work was also honored that year. She was nominated for an Emmy award, but it wasn't for *Drop Dead Diva*. Emmys are for the best work by people involved in the television industry. Cho's nomination was for her recurring appearances on the hit sitcom *30 Rock*.

Cho played Kim Jong-Il, the dictator of North Korea. Cho had her hair cut short and wore traditional man's clothing for the male role. She said, "I love that I get to play this character. To me, it's a very natural, easy thing to do and it's shocking to me how much I really look like him."[12] *30 Rock* creator Tina Fey said that casting Cho to play Kim was one of the standout moments of the many years *30 Rock* was on the air. The dictator wasn't referred to by name on the show. He was simply called Dear Leader.

On her blog, Cho mentioned how excited she was. But she also joked about her lazy and casual lifestyle and how she would have to get cleaned and dressed up to attend the televised awards competition. "I never really went to too many award shows, and I guess this is when I need to take a shower and put lotion on my feet."[13] Cho didn't win the Emmy. It was awarded to veteran character actress Kathy Bates. Still, the nomination did confirm that Cho is a talented actor.

Chapter 10

PRIDE

Cho's fame proved to be a gateway to even more opportunities. She was selected to be one of the contestants on the reality/talent show *Dancing with the Stars*. Early in the season, Cho told the audience that she had loved dancing when she was a kid, but stopped after someone called her a "fat ballerina."[1]

At every episode the couple with the lowest vote total has to leave the show. Cho was teamed up with a professional dancer named Louis Van Amstel. The duo made it through the first two episodes. For the third episode Cho and Van Amstel danced a samba. They had a week to practice. But unlike couples who could practice in the studio, Cho was traveling, doing "Cho

Pride

Dancing With the Stars

Dancing with the Stars first aired in 2005 and has been a very popular show. It sets up famous people ranging from actors to business leaders with professional dancers to compete in a weekly dance contest. Half of their scores come from a panel of judges. The other half is decided by the people watching from home. While it is a competition, it is also a fun show. The participants dance on a large floor. Most wear dazzling costumes while they dance to the music of a live orchestra. However, many participants who are not professional dancers often say while being on the show is fun, the practice sessions are often more difficult and tiring than they expected.

Dependent." So she and Van Amstel had to find time to practice whenever and wherever they could. They practiced on the tour bus, in parking lots, and even in hotel laundry rooms.

Cho wore a fringy, rainbow-colored dress and rainbow-colored socks. Van Amstel wore a rainbow belt. Their outfits were part of a theme that evening called "Story Night." All the contestants told stories that went with their dance choices. Cho and Van Amstel told the story of a gay coming-out party. It was in response to a series of news reports about LGBT people who felt so hopeless that they killed themselves. "We want this to end now," Cho firmly told ABC News.[2]

Margaret Cho: Comedian, Actress, and Activist

Cho was paired with professional dancer Louis Van Amstel on *Dancing with the Stars*.

Cho explained to correspondent Robin Roberts of the television show *Good Morning America*, "We wanted to tell a story that was really about pride. So my story is when I was a young person I felt so overweight that I wanted to die. So our dance is about the moment I felt good enough that to want to live. So I wanted to impart that message about pride to all kids out there."[3]

Van Amstel then went into more detail. "We wanted to show with [the rainbow outfits] that we are all living on this planet together and let's appreciate each others' differences and celebrate that fact that we're not the same. Otherwise, this planet would be quite boring."[4]

Unfortunately the duo finished that night with the lowest point total and had to leave the show. Cho was gracious in defeat. On *Good Morning America* she said, "It's all about pride and I'm so proud of our dance and what we got to do."[5]

By appearing on *Dancing with the Stars*, Cho was able to send her message about LGBT rights to millions of people who had previously known little about the cause. *Dancing with the Stars* is watched by millions who are not Cho's usual audience. Many who watched Cho dance had never heard of her before.

Branching Out

Being so driven, Cho continues to experiment with projects in new media. In January 2013 she began co-hosting a weekly podcast with comedian Jim Short. Its title is *Monsters of Talk*. During each podcast, Cho and Short interview writers, actors, musicians, and political activists. Then in 2014 she took part in what for her was a new style of film. It is a documentary titled *Do I Sound Gay?* It explores the stereotypes of what are seen as gay men's speech patterns.

A major change in Cho's personal life occurred in 2014. She and husband Al Ridenour decided to divorce. The *London Daily Mail* newspaper wrote, "The arrangement worked well for more than a decade but sadly for Margaret Cho her open marriage has come to an end."[6] Despite her unusual marriage situation, Cho found her divorce as difficult as people with traditional marriages find theirs. A friend said, "It's been really, really hard for her. She's going through a really rough time and she's really sad about it."[7]

The year 2014 also spelled the end for *Drop Dead Diva*. Its viewership had dropped steadily over the five years it had been on. In its first season, *Drop Dead Diva* had an average of 2.84 million viewers per first-run episode. By the fourth season that number had dropped to 2.3 million per episode. In the fifth season, it averaged 1.99 million. By losing viewers every year, the show was losing money. It would have been poor business sense for Lifetime to continue it. The last episode of *Drop Dead Diva* ran on June 22, 2014.[8]

Golden Globes Controversy

Because Cho had success depicting the Korean dictator on Tina Fey's sitcom *30 Rock*, she appeared in a similar role on the 2015 broadcast of the Golden Globe Awards.

PRIDE

Cho appeared as fictional North Korean general Cho Yung Ja at the 2015 Golden Globe Awards ceremony. She had played a similar role on *30 Rock*, lampooning real-life North Korean dictator Kim Jong-Il.

On January 11, 2015, Fey and her comedian friend Amy Poehler hosted the Golden Globes. The ceremony was televised live. At one point Fey and Poehler brought out someone they claimed to be the newest member of the Hollywood Foreign Press Association. It was Cho dressed as a fictional character named Cho Yung Ja. He claimed to be a North Korean army general who also was a journalist. Cho stood in a North Korean military

Golden Globe Awards

Golden Globe Awards are given every year to the best entertainers in television and film. Unlike other awards, the Golden Globes are noteworthy for their judges: members of the media from other countries (officially called the Hollywood Foreign Press Association). The Golden Globes were first awarded in 1944. In those days before television was a common medium, the awards were given only to film. In 1956, Golden Globes were first awarded to television shows. The Golden Globe movie winners are often seen as a preview of who might win the Oscar awards later in the winter.

uniform with an angry stone-faced expression. As in the past, her comments angered many people. But this incident was different from previous ones. This time it was liberals who accused her of racism.

When Fey and Poehler asked the dictator for an opinion of the show, Cho answered in a strong Korean accent that it isn't a fun show. She went into details, using stereotypes about life in North Korea. She even referenced NBA (National Basketball Association) great Dennis Rodman, who once paid an unofficial diplomatic visit to North Korea. Cho, in character as the journalist said, "In North Korea, we know how to put on a show." Cho-as-Korean-dictator continued, "This is not a show. You no have thousand baby playing guitar at the same time. You no have people holding up many cartoon to make one big picture. You no have Dennis Rodman. No basketball at all."[9]

Outraged liberals accused Cho of being racist. The editors at Vulture.com, a website devoted to pop culture, wrote, "That bit with Margaret Cho as the Kim regime's representative in the Hollywood Foreign Press, which managed a trio of awards-show sins: it was unfunny, racist, and incredibly long. Twenty years ago, Cho was the first Asian-American woman to headline her own sitcom—how did we end up here?"[10]

Cho responded to the critics on Twitter. She said that the routine was meant to be satire and the critics should lighten up. She tweeted the day after the broadcast that she was making fun of the current North Korean dictatorship. She wrote, "I'm of mixed North/South Korean descent—you imprison, starve and brainwash my people, you get made fun of by me."[11]

Anything but a "psy-CHO"

In 2015, she began a new comedy tour called "psy-CHO." She explained the meaning behind the title on the television talk show *The Real*. "When women are very outspoken about something, [people] go, 'Oh, she's just a psycho. Don't listen to her. She's just being hysterical.' So I wanted to actually use that word as a power word, that women's anger is really important right now."[12]

The "psy-CHO" show also allowed Cho to realize one of her dreams. A few years ago she was pleased to conduct LGBT weddings in San Francisco. Still, she hoped one day to be able to perform them everywhere. In June

Margaret Cho: Comedian, Actress, and Activist

Margaret Cho has found a way to merge comedy and activism. After several decades in show business, she shows no signs of stopping.

Pride

2015, same-sex marriage was legalized by the United States Supreme Court. That means it is legal in all fifty states. At the end of her "psy-CHO" tour performances, she invited same-sex couples to join her onstage. If they wanted to be married, she legally married them right there. Cho said, "At each tour stop, this is like the grand finale of the show."[13]

Chronology

1968—Margaret Moran Cho born on December 5 in San Francisco.

1984—Expelled from high school; attends School of the Arts (SOTA).

MID 1980s—Begins performing at area comedy clubs; performs on *Star Search International*.

1992—Appears on *Bob Hope's Ladies of Laughter* television special on November 28.

—Performs on *The Arsenio Hall Show*.

1994—*All-American Girl* premieres on September 14.

1995—Last episode of *All-American Girl* airs on May 15.

1999—"I'm the One That I Want" tour.

2000—*I'm the One That I Want* movie released.

2001—"Notorious C.H.O." tour.

2002—*Notorious C.H.O.* movie released.

2003—"Revolution" tour; marries Al Ridenour.

2004—*Revolution* movie released.

2005—*Bam Bam and Celeste* movie released; *I Have Chosen to Stay and Fight* book published; Stanley Tookie Williams campaign.

2007—Hosts "True Colors" tour.

2008—Margaret Cho Day in San Francisco; deputized to preside over same-sex marriages.

Chronology

2009—*Drop Dead Diva* premiers on July 12.

2010—"Cho Dependent" tour.

2011—Appears on *Dancing with the Stars*.

2011–2012—Appearances on *30 Rock*.

2014—Divorces Al Ridenour; last episode of *Drop Dead Diva* on June 22.

2015—Controversial appearance on Golden Globe Awards telecast; "psy-CHO" tour; legally presides over same-sex marriages throughout the country.

Chapter Notes

Chapter 1. A Wonderful Mother's Day Present

1. Margaret Cho, *I'm the One That I Want* (New York: Ballantine Books, 2001), p. 104.

Chapter 2. "They Hated Me"

1. Margaret Cho homepage, http://margaretcho.com/bio/ (accessed Oct. 14, 2015).
2. Margaret Cho, *I'm the One That I Want* (New York: Ballantine Books, 2001), p. 14–15.
3. Ibid., p. 47.
4. Ibid., p. 51.
5. Conor Murphy, "Margaret Cho to Bring Socially Aware Laughs," University of Wisconsin *Daily Cardinal*, Oct. 12, 2014, http://host.madison.com/daily-cardinal/margaret-cho-to-bring-socially-aware-laughs/article_f5455e96-5288-11e4-bb49-e3db319bc263.html (accessed Oct. 14, 2015).

Chapter 3. Joking Around with Batwing Lubricant

1. Margaret Cho, *I'm the One That I Want* (New York: Ballantine Books, 2001), p. 55.
2. Ibid., p. 62.
3. Ibid., p. 70.
4. Ibid., p. 71.
5. Tim Brooks and Earle Marsh, *The Complete Directory to Prime Time Network and Cable TV Shows (1946–Present)*, Ninth edition (New York: Ballantine Books, 2007), p. 1292.

Chapter 4. All-American Girl

1. Margaret Cho, *I'm the One That I Want* (New York: Ballantine Books, 2001), p. 99.
2. Margaret Cho Biography, Internet Movie Database, http://www.imdb.com/name/nm0158632/bio (accessed Oct. 14, 2015).
3. Kathleen Wilkinson, "The CHO Must Go On," EBSCOHOST, originally appeared in *Lesbian News*, June 2002, http://web.b.ebscohost.com/ehost/detail/detail?sid=fbf74a65-f04e-49cd-9e37-ceb303dc4492%40sessionmgr110&vid=0&hid=102&bd (accessed Oct. 14, 2015).

Chapter 5. Too Asian or Not Asian Enough

1. Margaret Cho, *I'm the One That I Want* (New York: Ballantine Books, 2001), p. 114.
2. Tim Brooks and Earle Marsh, *The Complete Directory to Prime Time Network and Cable TV Shows (1946–Present)*, Ninth edition (New York: Ballantine Books, 2007), p. 1694.
3. "Margaret Cho All American Girl, Pilot (1/2)" Youtube.com, https://www.youtube.com/watch?v=I4Q8HhKT3MY&list=PLhznUGv3fbfjqsYD-ZvG5DTzFZmj_KrZs (accessed October 31, 2015).
4. Ibid.
5. K. Connie Kang, "'Girl' Undergoes Major Changes Amid Criticism," *The Los Angeles Times*, Mar. 11, 1995, http://articles.latimes.com/1995-03-11/entertainment/ca-41514_1_korean-american (accessed Oct. 20, 2015).
6. E. Alex Jung, "All-American Girl at 20: The Evolution of Asian-Americans on TV," *Los Angeles Review of Books*, Nov. 9, 2014, https://lareviewofbooks.org/

essay/american-girl-20-evolution-asian-americans-tv/ (accessed Oct. 30, 2015).

7. Internet Movie Database, http://www.imdb.com/title/tt0108693/?ref_=fn_al_tt_1 (accessed Oct. 30, 2015).

8. Michelle Woo, "20 Years Later, Margaret Cho Looks Back on 'All-American Girl,'" *KoreAm*, Sept. 15, 2014, http://iamkorean.com/20-years-later-margaret-cho-looks-back-on-all-american-girl/ (accessed Oct. 30, 2015).

9. "Margaret Cho +Amy Hill: All American Girl Interview," *Youtube.com*, https://www.youtube.com/watch?v=AeWDsCyDLNw.

Chapter 6. "This Isn't Me. This is Stupid."

1. "New Apartment," Youtube video, https://www.youtube.com/watch?v=T1ilTtCg5tg (accessed Nov. 28, 2015).

2. "Margaret Cho and Amy Hill," Youtube video, https://www.youtube.com/watch?v=AeWDsCyDLNw&list=PLhznUGv3fbfjqsYD-ZvG5DTzFZmj_KrZs&index=10. (accessed Dec. 17, 2015).

3. Michelle Woo, "20 Years Later, Margaret Cho Looks Back on 'All-American Girl,'" *KoreAm*, Sept. 15, 2014, http://iamkorean.com/20-years-later-margaret-cho-looks-back-on-all-american-girl/ (accessed Oct. 30, 2015).

4. Margaret Cho Biography, Bestcomedyonline.com, http://www.bestcomedyonline.net/comedian-biographies/margaret-cho-biography-personal-life-career (accessed Dec. 15, 2015).

5. Paul Brownfield, "'All-American' Survivor," *The Los Angeles Times*, Feb. 1, 1999, http://articles.latimes.com/1999/feb/01/entertainment/ca-3719 (accessed Nov. 11, 2015).

CHAPTER NOTES

6. Margaret Cho, *I'm the One That I Want* (New York: Ballantine Books, 2001), p. 143.
7. Jason Lynch, "Cho Business," *People*, Mar. 10, 2003, http://www.people.com/people/article/0,,20139490,00.html (accessed Nov. 20, 2015).
8. Cho, pp. 196–197.
9. Ibid., p. 204.
10. "I'm the One That I Want (Live in Concert)," Youtube video, https://www.youtube.com/playlist?list=PLmhQWyZXQRbAh1jVx5DRC7Qoqd5UUDXwE (accessed Nov. 28, 2015).
11. Ibid.
12. Ibid.

Chapter 7. Lining Up Around the Block

1. "I'm the One That I Want (Live in Concert), Youtube video, https://www.youtube.com/playlist?list=PLmhQWyZXQRbAh1jVx5DRC7Qoqd5UUDXwE.
2. Leo Benedictus, "Comedy Gold: Margaret Cho: I'm the One That I Want," *The London Guardian*, May 10, 2012, http://www.theguardian.com/stage/2012/may/10/margaret-cho-one-i-want-comedy-dvd (accessed Nov. 11, 2015).
3. Ibid.
4. Dennis Harvey, "Review: 'I'm the One That I Want,'" *Variety*, July 5, 2000, http://variety.com/2000/film/reviews/i-m-the-one-that-i-want-2-1200463577/ (accessed Nov. 16, 2015).
5. "I'm the One That I Want," Internet Movie Database, http://www.imdb.com/title/tt0251739/?ref_=fn_al_tt_1 (accessed Nov. 16, 2015).
6. Greg Herren, "Fag Hag," EBSCOHOST, originally appeared in *Lambda Book Report*, July/Aug. 2001, http://web.b.ebscohost.com (accessed Oct. 14, 2015).

7. "Margaret Cho on Using the Name Notorious CHO," Youtube video, https://www.youtube.com/watch?v=1-JYHrKOgo4 (accessed Nov. 28, 2015).

8. Kathleen Wilkinson, "The CHO Must Go On," EBSCOHOST, originally appeared in *Lesbian News,* June 2002, http://web.b.ebscohost.com, (accessed Oct. 14, 2015).

9. "2002 Notorious C.H.O." Youtube video, https://www.youtube.com/watch?v=GciJwLUEORw (accessed Nov. 28, 2015).

10. Ibid.

11. Ibid.

12. Ibid.

13. Ibid.

14. Ibid.

15. Ibid.

16. David Noh, "Notorious C.H.O.," filmjournal.com, November 1, 2004, http://www.filmjournal.com/node/13512 (accessed Nov. 18, 2015).

17. Jeff Vice, "Film Review: Notorious C.H.O.," *Deseret News,* November 1, 2002, http://www.deseretnews.com/article/700003077/Notorious-CHO.html (accessed Nov. 18, 2015).

Chapter 8. "I Got Squid and Peanuts"

1. "Margaret Cho Opens Up About Her Open Marriage, Outing John Travolta," *Huffington Post,* Aug. 8, 2013, http://www.huffingtonpost.com/2013/08/08/margaret-cho-open-marriage_n_3727268.html (accessed Nov. 18, 2015).

2. Ibid.

3. Ibid.

Chapter Notes

4. "Margaret Cho Revolution Part 3." Youtube video, https://www.youtube.com/watch?v=wZw2f6RzjwI. (accessed Dec. 15, 2015).
5. Ibid.
6. David Rooney, "Review: 'Revolution,'" *Variety*, June 12, 2004, http://variety.com/2004/film/reviews/revolution-4-1200532867/ (accessed Nov. 22, 2015).
7. Margaret Cho: Revolution (review), flickfilosopher.com, July 26, 2004, http://www.flickfilosopher.com/2004/07/margaret-cho-revolution-review.html (accessed Nov. 22, 2015).
8. "Bam Bam and Celeste," imdb.com, http://www.imdb.com/title/tt0441737/ratings (accessed Nov. 22, 2015).
9. Rob Gonsalves, "Bam Bam and Celeste," efilmcritic.com, Oct. 6, 2007. http://www.efilmcritic.com/review.php?movie=12801 (accessed Nov. 24, 2015).

Chapter 9. The Activist

1. Margaret Cho, *I Have Chosen to Stay and Fight* (New York: Riverhead Books, 2005), p. 125.
2. Ibid., p. 29.
3. Ibid., p. 17.
4. Ibid.
5. Margaret Cho homepage, "R.I.P. Stanley Tookie Williams," Dec. 13, 2005, http://margaretcho.com/2005/12/13/rip-stanley-tookie-williams (accessed Nov. 29, 2015).
6. Cho, *I Have Chosen to Stay and Fight*, p. 6.
7. Ibid., p. 8.
8. Nate Chinen, "Power to the People (and Some Pop Too)" *The New York Times*, June 20, 2007, http://www.nytimes.com/2007/06/20/arts/music/20true.html?8dpc&_r=1 (accessed Nov. 29, 2015).

9. "True Colors Hollywood-Margaret Cho." Youtube video, https://www.youtube.com/watch?v=NWigtO-lTvM. (accessed Dec. 15, 2015).

10. Marc Malkin, "Deputy Margaret Cho Performing Gay Marriages," *Eonline.com*, July 10, 2008, http://www.eonline.com/news/2876/deputy-margaret-cho-performing-gay-marriages (accessed Nov. 29, 2015).

11. Stephanie Nolasco, "Q&A With 'Drop Dead Diva's' Margaret Cho," starpulse.com, June 4, 2010, http://www.starpulse.com/news/Stephanie_Nolasco/2010/06/04/qa_with_drop_dead_divas_margaret_cho (accessed Dec. 1, 2015).

12. "'30 Rock': Tina Fey Says Margaret Cho as Kim Jong Il Was One of Her Favorite Moments," *Huffington Post*, June 12, 2012, http://www.huffingtonpost.com/2012/06/12/30-rock-tina-fey-margaret-cho-kim-jong-il_n_1590327.html (accessed Nov. 30, 2015).

13. Margaret Cho homepage, "Emmy Nomination!!!," July 20, 2012, http://margaretcho.com/2012/07/20/emmy-nomination-2/ (accessed Nov. 30, 2015).

Chapter 10. Pride

1. "Dancing With the Stars: Tearful Margaret Cho Blasts Judges for Being Too Hard on Her as She Gets the Boot," *The Daily Mail*, Oct. 6, 2010, http://www.dailymail.co.uk/tvshowbiz/article-1318112/Dancing-With-The-Stars-2010-Margaret-Cho-blasts-judges-hard.html (accessed Nov. 30, 2015).

2. Lauren Sher, "'Dancing With the Stars': Margaret Cho Sent Home for Samba," abcnews.com (broadcast), Oct. 6, 2010, http://abcnews.go.com/Entertainment/dancing-stars-results-margaret-cho-louis-van-amstel/story?id=11810833 (accessed Nov. 30, 2015).

3. Ibid.

CHAPTER NOTES

4. Ibid.
5. Ibid.
6. Julie Moult, "Comedienne Margaret Cho 'to Divorce' Her Artist Husband After 11 Years of Open Marriage," *The Daily Mail*, Dec. 20, 2014, http://www.dailymail.co.uk/tvshowbiz/article-2882152/Comedienne-Margaret-Cho-divorce-artist-husband-11-years-open-marriage.html (accessed Nov. 20, 2015).
7. Ibid.
8. Lesley Goldberg, "Lifetime's 'Drop Dead Diva' to End After Sixth Season," *The Hollywood Reporter*, Feb. 13, 2014, http://www.hollywoodreporter.com/live-feed/lifetimes-drop-dead-diva-end-679973 (accessed Dec. 1, 2015).
9. "Margaret Cho mocks Kim jong-un at 2015 Golden Globes," Youtube video, https://www.youtube.com/watch?v=6Hia8yDMEo0 (accessed Dec. 1, 2015).
10. "The Highs and Lows of the 2015 Golden Globes," vulture.com, Jan. 12, 2015, http://www.vulture.com/2015/01/highs-and-lows-of-the-2015-golden-globes.html (accessed Dec. 1, 2015).
11. Ryan Gajewski, "Golden Globes: Margaret Cho Fires Back at Critics of North Korea Bit," *The Hollywood Reporter*, Jan. 12, 2015, http://www.hollywoodreporter.com/news/golden-globes-margaret-cho-fires-763194 (accessed Dec. 1, 2015).
12. "Margaret Cho on Her 'psyCHO' Tour & Girl Power," Youtube video, https://www.youtube.com/watch?v=rdsEXWu6vZw (accessed Dec. 2, 2015).
13. Ashley Lee, "Margaret Cho Explains Why She's Holding Gay Weddings on Her Psycho Comedy Tour," *The Hollywood Reporter*, July 25, 2015, http://www.hollywoodreporter.com/news/margaret-cho-holding-gay-weddings-826742 (accessed Nov. 29, 2015).

Glossary

agent—A person who represents actors and tries to get them jobs.

audition—The act of trying out for an acting role.

beauty contest—A competition in which a person is judged mainly on his or her appearances but also sometimes on his or her talent, poise, and character.

casting director—A person who auditions actors trying out for a role in a movie, television show, or play.

documentary—A nonfiction movie, often made to advocate a specific point of view.

gig—A job for someone in the entertainment business.

heckler—A person in the audience who insults or teases an entertainer while he or she is performing.

LGBT—A person who is lesbian, gay, bisexual, or transgender.

makeover—The act of improving a person's appearance by changing his or her hairstyle and clothing.

manager—One who helps entertainers make business decisions.

performance art—A complex form of art that is sort of a combination of art and acting.

personal trainer—A physical fitness expert hired to help a person get into better shape.

pilot—In television, a test episode of a new show.

screenplay—A movie script.

GLOSSARY

screen test—The act of an entertainer reading parts of a script in order to see how he or she will look when acting in a movie or television show.

Stand-up comedy—A style of performing in which a comedian tells jokes or funny stories onstage in front of a live audience.

stereotype—A belief in how a person will act based on his or her nationality, religion, race, or gender.

Supreme Court—The highest-level court in a state or nation.

television network—A company that produces programs to be broadcast over a group of stations it manages.

Further Reading

Books

Collins-Donnelly, Kate. *Banish Your Body Image Thief: A Cognitive Behavioral Therapy Workbook Building Positive Self-esteem for Young People*. Philadelphia, PA: Jessica Kingsley Publishers, 2014.

Foran, Racquel. *North Korea: Countries of the World*. Edina, MN: Abdo Group, 2013.

Foran, Racquel. *South Korea: Countries of the World*. Edina, MN: Abdo Group, 2013.

Gay, Kathlyn. *Activism: The Ultimate Teen Guide*. Lanham, MD: Rowman & Littlefield Publishers, 2016.

Gay, Kathlyn. *Bigotry and Intolerance: The Ultimate Teen Guide*. Lanham, MD: Scarecrow Press, 2015.

Lamedman, Debbie. *A Teen Drama Student's Guide to Laying the Foundation for a Successful Acting Career*. Hanover, NH: Smith & Kraus, 2014.

Osborne, Linda Barrett. *This Land Is Our Land: A History of American Immigration*. New York: Abrams Books for Young Readers, 2016.

Ryan, Aryna. *Creativity: The Ultimate Teen Guide*. Lanham, MD: Rowman & Littlefield Publishers, 2015.

Testa, Rylan Jay, Deborah Coolhart, and Jayme Peta. *The Gender Quest Workbook: A Guide for Teens and Young Adults Exploring Gender*. Oakland, CA: Instant Help Publications, 2015.

Further Reading

Websites

Kids n' Comedy
kidsncomedy.com
This New York City-based group offers stand-up comedy instruction to young people, as well as the opportunity to perform. Check out their website, even if you are not in the area.

Margaret Cho
margaretcho.com
Margaret Cho's official website offers Cho's blog, podcast, tour dates, and other information about the hilarious comedian. Note that some of the content might not be suitable for young audiences.

The Trevor Project
thetrevorproject.org
The Trevor Project provides crisis intervention for LGBTQ youth. The organization offers free guidance from volunteers and sponsors events for the LGBTQ youth community.

Index

A
ABC Network, 8, 9, 45, 47, 52, 53, 63
Academy Awards, 42
Aguilera, Christina, 36
All-American Girl, 8, 10, 45, 53, 54, 55, 56, 58, 59, 60, 61, 63, 66, 68, 69, 72, 98
Allen, Tim, 54
Amsterdam, Holland, 32
Arsenio Hall Show, The, 42

B
Bam Bam and Celeste, 88, 89, 90
Barr, Roseanne, 54
Batwing Lubricant, 28, 30
Big Bang Theory, The, 7
birth, 11
Bob Hope Presents the Ladies of Laughter, 43
Bush, George W., 91, 92
Butler, Brett, 54

C
California State Supreme Court, 97
Carnegie Hall, 77
Carolines on Broadway, 32
Carroll, Diahann, 58
Chappelle, Dave, 32
Cho Dependent, 100, 102-103
comedy clubs, 30, 32
Comedy Store, The, 32
Coulter, Ann, 91
Critic, The, 42

D
Dancing With the Stars, 102, 103, 105
DeGeneres, Ellen, 54
Destiny's Child, 36
Django Unchained, 83
Do I Sound Gay?, 106
Drop Dead Diva, 98, 101, 106
Dudley Stone School, 16

E
Ellen, 54

F
Fey, Tina, 32, 101, 106, 107
focus groups, 9

G
Godzilla, 39
Golden Globe Awards, 106, 107, 108
Golden Palace, The, 40, 42
Good Morning America, 105
Grace Under Fire, 54
Grammy Awards, 86, 88, 100

H
Haight-Ashbury, 11, 12, 13, 16, 17
hecklers, 38, 39

INDEX

Hollywood Foreign Press Association, 107, 108
Home Improvement, 54
Hope, Bob, 42, 43

I

I Have Chosen to Stay and Fight, 91, 92, 93
Improv, The, 32
I'm the One That I Want, 69, 74, 75, 77, 78
Internet Movie Database, 59, 89
Isaak, Chris, 83

J

Julia, 58

K

Kilgariff, Karen, 66
Korean Methodist Church, 17
Korean War, 79

L

Lauper, Cyndi, 95
Lifetime, 98, 106
London Guardian, 74
Lowell High School, 20, 22

M

M*A*S*H, 79
Merton, Robert K., 9
Modern Family, 7
Monsters of Talk, 105

N

New York City, 9, 69, 74, 77, 88
New York Times, The, 95
Notorious C.H.O., 75, 77, 82
Notre Dame Nursery School, 14-16

O

O'Donnell, Rosie, 36
Other Café, The, 30

P

Paperback Traffic, 20
Park, Lotte, 18, 19
Park, Connie, 18, 19
People Tree, The, 66
pilot episode, 8-9, 47, 50, 58
Poehler, Amy, 32, 107
psy-CHO, 109, 111
Pulp Fiction, 83
Punchline, The, 30

R

Revolution, 85, 86, 88
Ridenour, Al, 83, 106
Roberts, Robin, 105
Rock, Chris, 32, 36
Rose and Thistle, 33
Roseanne, 54

S

same sex marriage, 97, 111
Sandler, Adam, 32
San Francisco, 10, 11, 14, 27, 30, 34, 74, 97, 109

San Francisco State
    College, 22
School of the Arts (SOTA),
    24, 25, 26, 30, 32
Second City, 32
Seinfeld, 54
Seinfeld, Jerry, 54
Short, Jim, 105
sitcom, 7, 8
Spears, Britney, 36
Star Search, 34, 36
Star Search International, 36
summer stock theater, 22, 23
Sweetriver Saloon, 34, 39

T

Tarantino, Quentin, 83
30 Rock, 101, 106
True Colors, 95

U

United States Supreme
    Court, 111

V

Van Amstel, Louis, 102,
    103, 105
Vietnam War, 13

W

Westbeth, 70
Westbeth Theater Center, 69
Williams, Robin, 30
Williams, Stanley Tookie, 94